MW01107673

Crazy Love
The Love Series
Part One

Emma Keene

Copyright © 2013 Outfox Digital Publishing

All rights reserved.

ISBN: **1494292505**
ISBN-13: **978-1494292508**

This is a work of fiction. Similarities to real people, places, or events are entirely coincidental.

DEDICATION

This book is dedicated to my husband and our two dogs. They keep me sane while I write. Their distractions are always welcome. I love you three, you're the best family I could have ever asked for.

CONTENTS

ACKNOWLEDGMENTS

I would like to acknowledge all the hard work and hours put in by Outfox Digital Publishing. Thank you so much, you did a wonderful job and I can't wait to see what we can do together in the future.

CHAPTER ONE

I sift through the mail, which appears to be all bills, as I walk across the grass and climb the porch steps. I stop looking for an acceptance letter to open the front door.

"Mom, I'm home."

There's no response, but I know she's home. She is always home in the afternoon.

I set my backpack down by the stairs and plop down on the couch to finish looking through the mail. My heart races as I find the envelope I've been waiting for. My boyfriend, Mitch, is already committed to play for State next year.

We've been planning the rest of our lives together for the past six months. When things got more serious, halfway through junior year, we decided to attend the same school. Mitch was offered scholarships at a few schools out of state, but we decided that it would be best for my family financially if I went to State. I think Mitch secretly didn't want to be that far away from his parents, but he would never admit it.

The plan was for Mitch to play football and I would major in education. When we both graduated, we would get married and either move back to Greenville and

I would teach, or if he made it to the pros we would move to whatever city he needed to be in.

My fingers tremble as I flip the envelope over and tear it open. My eyes skip over the letterhead and move right to the most important part of the letter, the first paragraph.

We regret to inform you that based on your High school cumulative GPA and your SAT scores, you have not been accepted at this time. We wish you the best in furthering your education at another institution of higher learning and thank you for taking the time to apply.

The air leaves my lungs. I read the letter again. I can't believe it. Getting into State seemed like such a sure thing. Tears form in my eyes as I think about the future I had planned with Mitch.

The front door opens and I shove the rejection letter between the cushions of the couch and quickly wipe the tears from my eyes with my sleeve.

"How was your day?"

I turn to my mom as she sets her purse down on the table near the front door. I think about telling her. She deserves to know about the letter, I know that, but she was so proud of the fact that I was going to attend her alma mater and be a teacher just like her… I can't do it, not yet.

"Oh… it was just fine, just the normal stuff."

She sits down on the couch next to me and cracks a smile. I do my best to smile back, but I have no idea if she's buying it.

"It's amazing isn't it… you've got two days of school left and then before you know it, you and Mitch will be at State. I'm so excited, for you both."

I can't take it. I have to change the subject, otherwise I will spill the news about State and I need some more time to figure out what to do. That and I want to tell Mitch before I tell Mom.

"Where were you? You're always home at this time."

I really look at her for the first time since she came home and I notice she isn't dressed in one of her typical teaching outfits. In fact, she's wearing a dress that I don't recall ever seeing before. I can't remember ever seeing my mother in something so… revealing.

Her red dress, a color that only a young movie star would ever wear, reaches only halfway down her thigh and the cut in the front is low enough that her cleavage is showing. My eyes wander back up and she is blushing enough that her cheeks are almost the same color as the dress.

She clears her throat and fiddles with her cell phone.

"I… I stopped by the movie set in town for a few minutes after work."

Ugh. The movie set. I don't get what the big deal is. It's all everyone has been talking about for the past two months. I've heard of the director, Dexter Baldwin, but I've never seen any of his films. Mitch swears they are the best action movies and he acted like a schoolgirl when he found out that Dexter Baldwin would be in Greenville.

Everyone in the town had been visiting the various set locations, I guess in hopes of being plucked out of obscurity to fill some vacant role in the film. Apparently my mom is no different.

Before I can ask my mom what she was doing there, and why she is dressed like *that*, her phone vibrates. She glances down and jumps up from the couch.

"I better… get dinner ready… that was your father and he should be home soon."

I wrinkle my nose as she heads into the kitchen. Weird. He almost never texts. My best guess is that he is checking in to see if we need anything before he heads home from the mill.

My thoughts drift back to the rejection letter that is now stuffed between the cushions of the couch. I pull my phone out of my pocket and open my text conversation with Mitch. He should be home from the gym by now.

Hey, baby.

I hit send. While I wait for a reply I listen for my mom. When I hear the water in the kitchen turn on I pull the letter from State out of the couch and jump up. I grab my backpack and head upstairs. I go in my room and close the door, making sure to lock it and throw myself on the bed as tears start to flow from my eyes, again.

My phone chirps and I pull my face out of the pillow. There is already a wet spot on it. I sniffle and take a deep breath before looking at my phone.

Hey.

I take another deep breath and type out my reply.

How was the gym?

Good.

I need to tell him about State. My fingers hover over the keys. I can't bring myself to do it. Just like with my mom, I know that I will have to tell Mitch, but I think that I should tell him in person. Maybe that way he will be more supportive and can help me figure out what to do. Yeah... I need to see Mitch and then we can figure it out.

Are you free tonight?

I set my phone down, and using my sleeve, wipe away my ruined mascara. My phone chirps.

I'm busy right now. Do you want to come over later?

Ugh.

I hesitate. I want to see Mitch right now.... I know that if he says he can't, then he probably has a good reason. Ever since his dad left, Mitch and his brothers had been responsible for keeping the farm running.

Sure. I'll sneak out after my parents go to bed.

I toss my phone on the bed and look at myself in the mirror. I pull a tissue from the box on my desk and clean up the rest of my ruined makeup. My mom possesses the ability to tell if I've shed a single tear and I'm not ready to explain the source and level of my frustration to her and my dad.

I pull my earbuds out of my backpack and plug them into my phone. As the music flows through my ears, I put my head on my pillow and close my eyes. Part of me knows that everything will work out, but there is some doubt still in my mind. I know Mitch will know what to do.

~~~~

There is a faint knock on my door that wakes me. I reach for my earbuds, but they have already fallen out while I was apparently sleeping.

"Yeah?"

"Dinner is ready."

The creak of the wooden floor marks the retreat of my mom. I rub the sleep from my eyes and let out a yawn as I stretch. I glance at my alarm clock. It's already six. I can't believe that I slept for almost three hours. I didn't think I was tired, maybe it was more of an emotional exhaustion that led to my nap.

I head down the stairs and into the kitchen. My dad is already sitting down, spooning some mashed potatoes onto his plate. Mom is at the sink, filling up three glasses with water. I take my seat at the table and my dad passes me the green beans.

"Thanks."

He nods. Mom sits down and sets my water in front of me and reaches for the salad. It's a simple dinner, but she makes good food. There is also a roasted chicken sitting in the middle of the table. The smell reaches my nose and I realize how hungry I actually am.

"How was school?" Dad says.

I take a deep breath. I want to tell him about State, I really do, but I swallow and hold off.

"Fine."

I pass the green beans to Mom and she passes me the potatoes.

"Does it feel good to be almost done?" Mom says.

I nod as I serve myself some potatoes and reach for the chicken that my dad has just carved up.

"It does. I can't believe high school is almost over."

It's the truth. The last four years have really flown by. I've made and lost friends and learned more about life than I ever expected. I've always heard people say that high school was the best time of their life. I wouldn't go that far. It was good, but not that good.

"How was your day?" Mom asks.

I zone out as Dad starts to talk about work. I still, to this day, can't stay awake if I listen to him talk about the mill. As soon as he starts to talk about the different kinds of woods and different blades they use, he might as well be speaking a foreign language.

"Amy?"

I turn to my mom. My dad has a smile on his face. I guess they noticed that I had zoned out.

"Yeah?"

"I was just wondering if you had received your acceptance letter from State yet," Dad says.

Can I keep lying?

"No… not yet."

"Huh. That's weird. Jimmy, from work, his son, Nick, got his last week."

I shrug.

"Yeah, I don't know."

"Don't stress," Mom says. "I know you got in, there's no way they wouldn't accept you."

If only she was right. I want to cry. I want to tell them. It takes everything I have to just nod, force a smile and keep my mouth shut about State.

I notice for the first time that Mom changed her

clothes. I wrinkle my brow. She usually wears her teaching clothes until she gets ready for bed, but she has changed into something a little more… conservative. It's a long brown dress that has a high neck and looks more like something she would normally wear to work.

My mouth opens to ask her why she changed, but as the first word forms on my lips, Dad starts to speak.

"How was school today, honey?"

"Oh, just fine. Nothing out of the ordinary. Most of the kids are getting antsy for summer vacation to start."

"I notice you didn't include yourself in that."

She laughs. It's a running joke that she looks forward to summer as much as the kids do. I want to be a teacher because of her. Even though Dad and I tease her, she does love teaching and she's good at it.

"Yeah, it's been a long year."

CHAPTER TWO

I hear the water rushing through the walls to refill the toilet in my parents room. It's a sound that I have come to not notice, after so many years, unless I listen for it. I walk over to my bedroom door and turn the knob slowly while lifting it up slightly. It's the only way that I've found to open the door without the handle creaking loudly.

I peer down the hall, toward my parents room, and wait. The light creeping out from under their door disappears and I slowly close my door again. They should be asleep within a few minutes.

My phone chirps and I pick it up. Waiting for me is a text from Mitch.

You still coming over?

I smile. I know that after the shitty day I have had, Mitch is the only one that can really make everything alright. He will know how to fix it.

Yeah, my parents are just going to bed. I'll leave in a few minutes.

Can't wait to see you, babe.

A smile crosses my face. I feel better already.

After a few more minutes of waiting, I slowly slide the window in my bedroom up. It's still cool enough at night that my parents will have their bedroom window closed, so I don't have to be too quiet, but I still don't want to take any chances. I doubt they would be too receptive of me sneaking out to see Mitch, late at night, even though my eighteenth birthday is just a couple of months away.

I climb through the window and onto the roof. I slowly close the window and walk to the end of the roof. There is a big tree on the far side of the house, with a large enough branch that I can reach out and get into the tree. From there, I just climb part way down the tree and drop the last couple of feet to the ground. I have done it a few dozen times now, usually when I want to see Mitch past curfew and the hardest part is actually climbing back up the tree to sneak back in.

Once I'm clear of the house, I brush the remnants of the tree from my shirt and start to walk faster. I should have brought a coat. I speed up with the hope that it will help me warm up a little. Not to mention it's almost a mile to Mitch's and I'm really looking forward to seeing him.

The roads are quiet and only one car passes me on my way to Mitch's house. I'm happy when I get there. The temperature has continued to drop and I'm feeling chilled. I should ask Mitch to borrow a hat, or something, for the walk home.

One of the main reasons we hang out at Mitch's house late at night is that his room is in what used to be the cellar of the farmhouse, so there is a separate entrance. It makes it easier. I don't have to jump off any roofs or climb trees, but we still try to be quiet, there's no point in waking up his brothers or his mom.

I knock on the door which opens and I step inside. Mitch closes the door and turns to me. He smiles. I return it as he lunges forward and lifts me off the floor. He pushes his lips against mine and sets me back down.

"It's so good to see you," I say.

"Yeah, it's good to see you, too."

Mitch takes my hand in his and leads me over to the couch that sits along the back wall of his room. I feel a little sad. We've grown so much, together, and spent so much time down in his room. I'm going to miss it.

We sit on the couch and he turns to me.

"So, what's up?"

I open my mouth, but nothing comes out. It doesn't make any sense. He should be the one person that I have no problem telling what is really happening.

"Amy, what is it? Is everything OK?"

I look into his eyes as tears start to form in my eyes. A look of worry crosses his face.

"What happened?"

"I got… I got a letter from State today."

Mitch is quiet. As I look at his face, I can see that he understands what happened. I feel relieved that someone else knows. Now we have to figure out what to do. I know Mitch will know what to do, he always does.

"Shit."

I nod. That sums up my thoughts pretty well.

Mitch leans closer to me and wraps his strong arms around me and I rest my head on his shoulder. He strokes my head with his right hand as I continue to cry. He kisses the side of my head.

He pulls back, puts his hands on my face and looks at me. I finally raise my eyes and meet his gaze. Mitch smiles at me. Even though I can tell it's forced, I still appreciate the effort. I do my best to smile back at him. He leans toward me and presses his lips to my forehead.

I sniffle as the last of my tears drip down my cheek and fall on the couch. Mitch reaches up and wipes the wetness from my eyes.

"It's going to be OK."

I nod. I don't believe him. It's not going to be OK, everything is ruined. Our whole plan is ruined.

"Maybe they made some kind of mistake," he

says.

The thought had crossed my mind. The more I think about it though, the more I realize that it was very unlikely and realistically they didn't make a mistake. State probably has what they believe to be justification for it. It just still seems surreal.

"I don't know what to do."

"What did your mom and dad say?"

"I haven't told them."

Mitch looks surprised.

"I couldn't do it," I say. "I really wanted to tell them, but I didn't want them to be disappointed in me."

"They wouldn't be. You're an only child… nothing you do would disappoint them."

I wrinkle my nose. That was a strange thing for Mitch to say.

"I guess I should have told them."

"You really should have. You should have told them right away. Now they are going to wonder why you waited to tell them."

"What are we going to do? You start school there in a few months… and now… now I don't know what I'm going to do."

Mitch stands up and starts to pace. I realize that Mitch is right. I should have told my parents first. Since it's too late for that now, I hope that he can help me figure out what we should do next. Thoughts of losing Mitch cross my mind. I know it won't come to that, but I can't stop myself from thinking about it. I force the thoughts out of my mind and just watch him as he walks back and forth, with a determined look on his face.

"OK… what did the letter say was the reason?"

"It said that my GPA and SAT score wasn't high enough."

Mitch stops and frowns and then sits down. He looks exactly how I felt when I first read the letter. It's still hard to believe. I feel sad and a little irritated, not exactly at

17

Mitch, but with the fact that he got into State with a lower GPA and SAT score because he plays football. It bugs me a little, I can't deny that, even though I know that's how it works. I instantly regret not spending more time studying… more time doing homework.

This is one of those moments. A moment that I know I'll look back on for the rest of my life and wish I could have done something more.

"Hmm. Well, I'm not sure what to do… but I promise we will work something out."

I take a deep breath. Calm down, Amy. Mitch is right. There's no reason to get so worked up over this.

Mitch sits back down on the couch and looks at me. He takes my chin in his hand and gently lifts it up so that my eyes meet his. There is a soft warmth in his face. I know he is going to take care of me.

"Let me think about what we should do. For now, just try to not think too much about it, but you should probably tell your parents. They might have an idea of what we should do, too."

I smile at Mitch. He's always been so good to me. It's almost hard to believe. At times I wonder what I did to deserve such a good boyfriend.

Mitch runs his fingers down the side of my cheek and I grab his hand and kiss the top of it. He smiles at me and motions for me to come closer. I scoot over and put my head on his chest and close my eyes.

~~~~

My eyes slowly open and it takes me a moment to realize where I am. When it hits me, I start to panic.

There is light coming through the windows of the basement. I pull out my phone and check the time, but it's dead. If I had to guess, based on the light coming into

Mitch's room, it would have to be after seven. Crap. I'm usually up and in the shower by now. A thousand thoughts rush through my mind. I turn to Mitch, who is still asleep and I start to shake him.

"Ugh…."

"Mitch, wake up… right now. I'm in trouble."

He cracks his eyes and sits up straight when he realizes that it's already light out. I jump off the couch and he follows. Mitch pulls a hoodie on and grabs his keys as we dash out the door.

We head for his truck and don't look back. I hope that his mom isn't up. We hop in and he's got the engine started before I can close my door.

Neither of us speaks a word. I watch the world pass as Mitch speeds down the road toward my house. As far as I'm concerned, every second matters, so I don't mind him driving a little faster than I'm usually comfortable with. He stops his truck near my house, right before the last turn and I hop out without so much as a goodbye. I'll see him at school.

I run to the back of my house, ducking as I pass the windows on the side where the kitchen is. I don't know if my parents are in there yet, but I don't want to take the chance. I jump and grab a branch and start to pull myself up the tree. The crisp morning air fills my lungs as I pause, take a deep breath, and jump from the branch onto the roof. The loud thump of my feet landing makes me cringe. I rush to my window, slide it open and duck inside. As I pull the window closed, and kick off my shoes at the same time, my bedroom door opens and I freeze.

"We need to talk," Mom says.

Before I can even begin to formulate a response in my mind, my door is closed again and she is gone. My heart starts to race.

I'm so screwed. A thousand thoughts race through my brain. I'll probably be grounded and there's no way that I can tell my parents about State, now, they would freak out and be even more disappointed in me.

Dragging my feet as I walk, I leave my room and head downstairs to face the firing squad. I step into the kitchen and my parents stop mid sentence and look at me. It's a weird feeling, almost like I'm a toy that is being inspected for faults. They are trying to decide if I pass and get to move on with my existence or I fail and get tossed to the bottom of a trash bin.

Dad motions for me to take a seat across the table from him. My mom gets up and stands at the sink, looking out the window. I can already tell this isn't going to be good. I hang my head and wait for it to begin.

"Where were you?"

I swallow and turn to my dad. He looks disappointed, but compared to the look on my mother's face, he looks calm and collected. I shouldn't be surprised, he's always been the one who steadies the ship when the waves start.

"I… I went to Mitch's house."

My mom starts to cry. I instantly feel bad, even though I'm not sure why my sneaking out would cause her to be upset emotionally. I get that she's mad, however, this is not the response I was expecting.

Why would me going to Mitch's house make her cry? It really makes no sense. My dad lets out a deep sigh and drums his fingers on the table.

"What were you doing there?"

I wrestle with telling them the truth. They are going to be pissed either way. Maybe I should just tell them about State. I take a deep breath and ready myself, emotionally, to deal with the slew of questions and judgment that is sure to follow.

"Yesterday, I got a letter from State…."

"Why didn't you tell us?" Mom says, interrupting me before I can finish.

I glare at her. She frowns and the look in her eyes tells me that she is sorry.

"I didn't say anything… well, because I didn't get in. It was a rejection letter."

She gasps and walks out of the room. The back door slams and she is gone. I put my hands on my face and take a deep breath. Don't cry Amy, not now.

"Sweetie, you should have told us."

He gets up and walks over to me and rests his hand on my shoulder.

"It's going to be OK. In the grand scheme of things, this is just a minor setback. I know you'll go on to do great things. You're my daughter, how could you not?"

I drop my hands and do my best to smile at him. He smiles back. His is genuine. I can see the love he has for me.

"And don't worry about your mother. I'll talk to her."

"Thanks Dad."

I stand up. It's getting late and I've gotta get ready for school.

"Now, go get ready. I'll drive you to school so that you aren't late."

I wrap my arms around him and squeeze. He kisses the top of my head and I dash off. He's right, I'm going to be late if I don't hurry.

CHAPTER THREE

I can't believe it. This is the last day I'll every walk home from high school. A smile crosses my face. It feels weird and good at the same time. It almost doesn't feel real. I have a feeling that when fall rolls around and I'm not going back to school in my hometown, it will finally seem real.

Thinking about school makes me sad. Not leaving high school… that's whatever. No, it's the fact that I'm not going to State with Mitch in the fall that has me in a funk. Thankfully none of my friends said anything over the last few days of school. I guess most of them just assumed I would be going, and I didn't feel like bringing it up.

Mitch has been sweet the last two days. He asked if I made home OK and if I told my parents. I didn't lie to him, but I didn't quite tell him the truth. I didn't mention my parents busting me while trying to sneak back in and I didn't tell him that my mom ran out when she found out about State.

My train of thought is broken when I hear several guys yelling.

"Yeahhhhh!"

I look up. I recognize the truck from school. I'm

not sure whose it is. There are two guys standing in the bed, with their hands planted on top of the cab, yelling as they speed down the road and blow by me.

I shake my head. Boys. And I thought I was excited to be graduating. The funny thing is that most of them will spend the rest of their lives in our little town, talking about how great high school had been.

My mom's car isn't in the driveway when I get home. It was weird the first day and strange yesterday. Today it is starting to bother me for some reason. I can't explain why though. I haven't talked to her since yesterday morning, but I wonder why she isn't home. I guess I'm mostly just curious as to where she could possibly be.

I head inside, set my backpack down at the base of the stairs, for the last time, and head into the kitchen to grab a snack. As I reach for the handle of the fridge, there is a knock on the front door. I let out a sigh. Of course, why wouldn't there be someone at the door right when I'm feeling hypoglycemic.

When I swing the door open, a large bouquet of lilies is thrust into my face by what I can only guess is another human being, but the flowers are blocking out my entire field of vision.

Without a word, the flower delivery person has left and I'm standing in the doorway, with what has to be the largest bouquet ever made. I back into the house, doing my best to not damage any of the flowers and shut the front door. I set it on the coffee table in the living room and take a step back.

There's something about lilies that I don't like. They remind me too much of death. My mom loves them though. I could never understand why. Every time I see lilies I think of my grandma's funeral, my mom's mom, who died when I was five.

As I stand looking at the flowers, trying to figure out what to do with them, the front door opens and my mom walks through. She pushes past me and pulls a card out of the flowers.

"Who are they from?"

She doesn't answer.

"Mom, who sent the flowers?"

When she doesn't answer a second time, I know she heard me and is choosing not to answer me. Whatever. I give up, grab my backpack and head up the stairs, and leave her standing in the living room.

I toss my backpack down on my bed and plop down next to it. I'm just glad I don't have to carry it anymore. It was particularly heavy today after cleaning out a year's worth of junk that accumulated in my locker. I pull the zipper, turn the bag upside down and dump it all out on my bed. I might as well go through it all right now, seeing as Mom is in some sort of a weird mood.

Most of the stuff from my locker is set into a pile of stuff to save, that I need to find a place for, although most of it will probably end up sitting on my desk in a pile, even though it should be in the trash. I just can't bear to throw out anything that I might regret.

A smile crosses my face, a real one, for what seems the first time in days as I look back at pictures of my friends and me from the year that I put up in my locker. The smile fades when it sinks in that most of them will be heading off to college in just a couple of months and I will be here, stuck in our hometown, alone.

My cell chirps and I pull it out of my pocket. A text from Mitch instantly improves my mood.

Hey. How are you?

Better now. Did you just get home from the gym?

I used to think he was crazy, when we first started dating, because he goes to the gym every day, but when he told me about his dreams to play football professionally it made sense. I'm proud of him. He's worked so hard to get where he is and I know that he will do his best at State.

Yeah. Are you coming tomorrow?

If it was anyone else, I wouldn't go. I had been

looking forward to his graduation party, as had most of the kids in school, but now... now that I wasn't going to State I almost didn't think anything was worth celebrating.

I am. Should I bring anything?

I set my phone down and pick up the picture from the top of the stack. It's of Mitch and me. We look cute together. A tear forms in my eye. He told me everything is going to work out between us and with me going to college, but I don't know if it will. I have some serious doubt in my mind. My phone chirps, again.

Nah, I'm going to help my mom right now. She's already started to cook. It's going to be a lot of fun. I can't wait to see you.

I can't wait either. Xoxo.

I want to believe that everything will work out. I want to trust in what my dad has said and what Mitch has told me, but I just don't know anymore. I get up from my bed to open my window. I need some fresh air.

I see my mom walking through the yard with the massive bunch of lilies in her arms. I wonder what she's doing. She quickly glances over her shoulder and heads for the gate at the back of the yard. She opens the gate and disappears into the grove of trees that starts just past our fence. I watch until I see her come back. The flowers are gone. I move away from the window. I don't really want her to know that I saw what she did, although I already know of the existence of the flowers.

It crosses my mind that she wouldn't throw away perfectly good flowers if they were from Dad, and I know things have been tight financially lately so I'm pretty sure he wouldn't have spent the kind of money that a bouquet that size would have cost. My mind races as I try to figure out who sent them and why she didn't want them.

The only thing I could think of is that someone sent them to her and she doesn't want Dad to find out. But who could they be from?

I don't know why I care. She hasn't spoken to me for days and I feel more disconnected from her than I ever have. I do my best to stop thinking about her and go back to sorting through the pile of papers and half-used school supplies from my locker. It's funny to think that I will never use that locker again, the same locker I had for four years, and someone else will get it in the fall and will have no idea how much of my life took place in and around that metal box.

With the rest of the stuff from my locker sorted, I get off my bed and toss the pile that is garbage in the can under my desk. I look around the room. It feels weird. For the last few months, I imagined myself graduating and then slowly packing up my room—boxes that would be going to college with me and boxes that would be left behind and stored in the attic until I was ready to move into my own house with Mitch and get married.

The idea of starting a new chapter in my life was so promising. It's still hard to believe that it was so close, I could feel it, and then it was ripped away from me.

I finish putting away what I want to keep, from my locker, and lie down on my bed. I wrap my arms around my pillow and close my eyes. I have to be tough, I know that. There's really no other way around it. Life isn't going to get any easier and it's probably going to get harder before anything changes.

CHAPTER FOUR

I roll over, shut off my alarm, and press my face back into my pillow. Ugh. It's way too early to be awake, especially on a Saturday.

One of the things I hate most about the weather getting warmer in May is that I have to open my window. I'm grateful for the airflow, but I have to leave my blinds open for it to make a difference and as soon as the sun comes up I'm up too and I hate it.

I groan and push myself up and rub the sleep from my eyes. A peek at my alarm clock reveals it's just past eight. Normally, I wouldn't mind waking up early, but my night wasn't exactly filled with sleep. I spent most of the night worried about what I was going to do with my life. It already feels like I'm drifting along.

It takes some effort, but I finally make myself get up. I put on my bathrobe, slippers, and head downstairs. Every Saturday, for as long as can remember, by the time I got downstairs, Mom was making, or had made, breakfast and Dad was getting ready for work. Today was different though.

When I stepped into the kitchen, it was just my dad. He was standing over the stove, something I was not used to seeing. He must have known that because he turned around and smiled when he saw the look on my face.

"What? You think your old man can't make pancakes?"

I smile at him. My favorite.

"No, I'm just used to Mom doing the cooking."

The look on his face turns from happy to sour and he turns back to the stove. I wrinkle my brow and decide not to ask.

I open the fridge and pull out the orange juice and set it on the table and put out plates and silverware for the three of us.

"Your mom isn't having breakfast. She… she isn't feeling well today."

"Is she OK?"

I put a plate back into the cabinet and put away the fork and knife.

"Yeah, I think she has a stomach flu or something."

Dad sets the plate of pancakes in the middle of the table and we take our seats. I pour myself some orange juice and then a glass for him.

"Thanks."

"Thank you, for making pancakes."

We smile at each other as we start to eat.

"Mmm. These are *really* good, Dad. Where did you learn to make pancakes?"

"Well, I did survive before I met your mother. I mostly just ate pasta and pancakes, but I lived long enough to meet her."

I let out a giggle. He could always make me smile. Not even my foul mood could change that. It was starting to bother me how distant Mom was being though. I could only assume that it was because I snuck out. She had been mad at me before, obviously, but this was worse. It almost seems like there was no end in sight and that unless I do something to make her proud again she might never speak to me. I know it's stupid. I wonder what I could do.

"You good?"

I look down and notice that my plate is empty. I ate three pancakes already. I nod as my dad gets up and starts to clean the kitchen.

"You should go get ready. We have to leave in… forty minutes or so. You can't be late for your own graduation."

Ugh. He's right. I don't even want to go anymore. A few weeks ago, I was really looking forward to today, and the party at Mitch's, and now… now I just want to curl up in a ball and die. I need to get through today without anyone finding out about State, that's the last thing I need.

I go upstairs, take a quick shower and throw on a T-shirt and comfy shorts. I put my hair up in a ponytail and grab my cap and gown out of the closet. I head downstairs and find Dad sitting in the living room, waiting for me.

"Should I tell Mom that we're going?"

He shakes his head and stands up.

"Nah. She's probably asleep anyway. I don't want to bother her."

I know he's right. Not to mention I don't want to put her in an even fouler mood.

We head outside and get in his car. For the first few minutes, we sit in silence.

"So, any ideas of what you want to do next?"

I've been trying not to think about it. I can't tell him that though, not after how supportive he was when I told him about State.

"I was thinking maybe a summer job and then community college."

"That's a good plan. I'm actually a little surprised that you've thought about it that much. If I were you, I would've tried to not think about it right now and just take it day by day."

I guess I still underestimate my dad. He really is a sweet man. I feel like no matter what I do, he will always love me. I want to feel that same way about my mom, I really do, but after the last couple of the days… I really don't know anymore.

We go back to driving in silence and I think more about Mom. I remember a few years ago, I can't remember what it was that I did, she was so mad that she didn't talk to me for two days and the only reason she finally did was that my parents had a huge argument. I had cried myself to sleep that night as they yelled, pushing my face into my pillow and covering my ears.

I start to wonder if my mom ever really wanted me. My parents had me in their early twenties and they never seemed that keen on having another kid, as far as I could tell.

Dad pulls the car into the teeming parking lot and turns off the engine. I get out and put on my cap and gown while he pulls out his camera. I take a deep breath and try to collect my thoughts. I focus on the present, everything else can wait. We walk to the football field, where the graduation ceremony was to be held.

I did my best to smile as we took our seats and waiting for the ceremony to start.

The first part of the ceremony is boring, just speeches by the valedictorian and the principal, and I tune it all out. My gaze, and my thoughts, are on the clouds. I watch as the puffs of white dance, effortlessly, across the blue sky, changing shape as they move. It makes me long to be free, but instead I feel trapped. Trapped in this town. A sick feeling fills my stomach. What if I never leave here?

My dad elbows me, gently, and I look up.

"Now, we need all graduates whose last name starts with a through j to please come to the stage and form a line."

I look over at my dad. He is tinkering with his

camera, getting ready to take my picture as I cross the stage. I smile. He's more excited than I am. If it weren't for him, I don't know that I would have even bothered to go.

It seems like an eternity before it's my turn to cross the stage. When I finally do, I look out into the crowd and locate my dad. He is standing, with his camera in front of his face. I force myself to smile as I take my diploma from the principal and walk off the stage.

There is a table set up on the far end of the stage where I wait, again, and hand the diploma over to one of the women who works in the office. In return, she hands me my actual diploma, the one with my name on it, and instructs me to head back to my seat.

I hand over the diploma, to my dad, as I sit down. His face lights up as he reads the whole thing. He gives it back to me and wraps his arms around me.

"I'm so proud of you," he says, whispering into my ear.

Even though she's still not talking to me, there is a part of me that wishes Mom could have been here.

When the graduation ceremony is finally over, we head back to the car.

"Do you mind if I drop you off at Mitch's? I want to go home and check on your mom."

"Sure. Of course."

We don't talk until we reach Mitch's house.

"Just call when you're ready for me to come pick you up."

"I can get a ride, or walk, it's not that big of a deal."

"Alright, but if you want me to come get you, just call."

I take off the gown and toss it on the back seat, on top of the cap, and close the passenger door of his car. I stand on the curb and watch as he turns around down the street and I wave to him as he drives by. He doesn't wave back. I don't think he even saw me. His mind must be a million miles away. If I know him, he's probably worried about Mom.

I hope she's alright.

The music blaring from Mitch's back yard draws my attention back to reality and I put a smile on my face as I walk around the side of the house. I'm going to try to have fun. I don't know if I'll be able to, but I promise myself that I will try.

Once I make it to the back yard, I'm greeted by the smiles of many of my classmates that have just graduated, many of them ready to party, but I don't stop to exchange passe pleasantries. I want to see Mitch. I finally spot him, by the food table, where there is a group of people gathered around him, mostly what looks to be members of his extended family that came to town for his graduation, so I lean against a tree and wait my turn.

Every few minutes, one of the family members moves and I catch a brief glimpse of Mitch, and each time I wave to try and get his attention, but he doesn't notice me after three tries so I give up.

Defeated, I look around and do some people watching. Everyone seems so happy. It's kind of weird. Usually I would be right there with them, laughing and having a great time, but it all seems so pointless now. I feel like I have nothing to look forward to. Thank god for Mitch. If I didn't have him I don't know what I would do.

"Hey, Amy."

I turn to the voice I don't recognize. I think his name is Ned. I'm not sure though, I've never actually talked to him, but going to a school the size of mine, it was hard to not at least have some idea of who everyone was. He smiles at me and pushes his glasses back up his face. They instantly slide back down and come to a rest right on the edge of his slightly upturned nose.

"Hey."

I'm not sure what to say to him.

"So, are you looking forward to State?"

Blegh. The thought of *State* made me sick. I didn't want to talk about what my life was turning into, not with anyone and definitely not with Ned.

"Yeah… I'm really excited."

"Me too! I can't sleep at night. It's going to be so amazing."

I nod. I want to scream. I want to grab him and shake him. I feel a hand come to rest on my shoulder and I turn around. It's Mitch and he hands me a red, plastic, cup and gives me a kiss on the cheek.

"What did he want?"

I turn back around, but Ned is gone and I don't see him anywhere. Weird.

"I have no idea."

"What a weirdo," Mitch says.

I wrinkle my forehead at him.

"What? He's a total nerd. He was on the chess team."

"I didn't know we even had a chess team," I say.

Mitch laughs.

"He was the only one on it. What a freak."

Mitch's hostility toward Ned is strange and making me feel uncomfortable. I take a sip out of my cup, which turns out to be punch, and look past him at the food table.

"I'm hungry."

I walk past Mitch, toward the table and set down my cup and pick up a plate. I'm not really hungry. I actually don't have an appetite at all, but I wanted to get out of that conversation. Mitch, who was always kind and nice to people, was acting strange.

The thought crosses my mind that Mitch could possibly be jealous of Ned, in some way, but it sounds crazy.

I put some potato salad and a roll on my plate and take a seat at one of the folding card tables. People I've known for years walk past me to get food, not even glancing in my direction, and I suddenly feel very alone. And invisible. I want to run away. I want to leave all this behind.

CHAPTER FIVE

A door slamming, somewhere in the house, wakes me up. I feel tired still and it doesn't register right away.

Another night of crappy sleep. The lack of sleep isn't helping my mood and my mood is affecting my sleep. Something needs to change.

I wonder why a door would be slamming at whatever time it is. I look at my alarm clock. The glaring red letters show twenty past five. I close my eyes and try to fall back asleep. There's something telling me to get up. I don't listen to myself.

The next time I open my eyes, it's almost six. I finally get up, knowing that my curiosity is getting the better of me. I didn't hear my parents yelling, and it would have woken me up if they were, so I have no idea what the door slamming was about.

I put on a shirt and shorts and head downstairs. Before I reach the bottom of the stairs, the smell of coffee reaches me. Weird. Mom doesn't drink coffee and Dad only drinks it when he has to work and it's Sunday, his only day off. Maybe he picked up an extra shift at work. I head into the kitchen, but he isn't around.

"Dad?"

There's no response. Maybe he left for work already. I open the front door, to go check if his car is in the driveway, and I see him, sitting on the front steps. His head is in his hands and his back is heaving, quickly, as if he is crying.

"Dad?"

His body becomes rigid, but he doesn't turn around.

"Yeah?"

"What's going on?"

He doesn't answer. I look toward the driveway and notice that Mom's car is gone. Where would she possibly have gone at six o'clock on a Sunday?

"Is everything OK?"

He stands up, turns around and wipes the remaining tears from his eyes.

"It's your mom… she left."

"What do you mean? Where did she go?"

He shakes his head and looks away from me. He looks like he was about to cry again. There isn't a single time in my entire life that I remember seeing him cry. He has always been emotionally strong. I start to panic. If he's this upset, something must have really been wrong.

"What happened? Did someone die or something?"

I hope that he can't sense the panic in my voice. The last thing he needs is for me to be stressed out, and I know that.

He lifts his head and I can see the pain in his eyes. He looks as if his will to live has been crushed under the weight of the world. He quickly looks away and walks past me, into the house. I don't go inside right away. I want him to be able to settle down, to figure out exactly what is going on, and then maybe he can really explain what happened with Mom. It's selfish, but I hope he doesn't take too long, because I feel like I'm about to start freaking out.

When I do finally go inside, I don't find him downstairs and just as I get ready to call out to him I hear my parents' bedroom door closing. I need to get out of here. I'm not sure what he needs right now, but he clearly wants to be alone. I decide to go for a walk, maybe into town, which could help me clear my head, too. I grab my sunglasses and purse out of my room, slip on some sneakers and head out.

The sun is finally coming up as I walk down the road I've spent my whole life living on. There's just something about it that is beginning to bother me. It's almost as if it has become too familiar. The more I think about it, the more I realize I'm not only upset about State because I don't get to go to college with Mitch, but that I also need to get out of this town.

When I reach Main Street, about thirty minutes after leaving home, it's empty. It seems odd. For the first time in months, there aren't people anymore. It looks like the movie crews have packed everything up and gone back to Hollywood. The occupation of our town has ended. I'm sure people in town will be sad, they all seemed to love it. I'm glad they are all gone, it made life in our small town seem big and made getting anywhere exceedingly difficult.

I walk to Java Stop and take a seat at one of the outside tables and wait for Nancy, the owner and sole employee, to come out and take my order.

"Hey Hun, what can I get you?"

"I'll have a latte and a muffin."

"Blueberry, banana nut or chocolate?"

"Chocolate."

Nancy nods and disappears back into the shop. What the heck, might as well go big or go home. Not to mention, chocolate always makes me feel better. I hope the coffee calms me down, too.

"It's crazy, isn't it?"

I turn my attention, from staring off into space, to Nancy. I have no clue what she's talking about.

"Yeah, sure is."

"It was my best three months, having those Hollywood people here. Even had to hire some additional staff. Oh well."

She sets the latte and muffin down in front of me and she heads back inside. For some reason, I feel irritated that she misses the film crew and I know that she won't be the last person to talk about it. I don't get it. The few people I met, who were just regular members of the crew, not actors or anything, they seemed so... so phony. I have this picture in my head now, that everyone in Hollywood is like that. It used to have some sort of romanticized appeal, to me, but that's gone.

I rip the plastic wrap off my muffin and break off a piece of the top. I love muffin tops, they are so much better than the bottoms. I never could figure that out. I alternate between bites of the delicious muffin and sips of my latte. Nancy makes the best coffee. I've never been a fan of those big coffee chains. I get the appeal, but I guess it's the small town girl in me that wants to support a business where the owner cares about the customer.

Once the muffin is gone I down the rest of my latte and put five dollars on the table for Nancy. It's more than my bill, but I want to get out of here. I walk the rest of the way down Main, and just keep walking. I have no idea where I'm going, but I have no reason to head home. Dad will probably still be in his room and I need to figure out what I'm doing.

I head toward the bike path that leaves town and parallels the highway. The path is empty, not that it's ever really busy, but it's nice to be able to walk alone and not have to dodge people on bicycles or runners.

The trees were finally starting to bloom, as were the flowers along the path and for a few minutes, while I walked, I almost forgot about my crappy week. Almost.

I need to figure out what to do.

The more I think about it, the more sense my spur

of the moment plan makes. Maybe I should stick around here, get a summer job and then go to community college in the fall. I know there's one not too far from State, it's where all the other rejects go. I should fit right in. At least that way I can have some semblance of a college experience and still be close to Mitch. If I work my ass off, I might be able to transfer to State after a few semesters.

Yeah. That's what I should do. Even though I do live in a small town, there are enough businesses that I should be able to get something. Maybe I can even save up enough to buy myself a car, something cheap and used. That would make life much easier. That way I could come home on weekends, or at least on holidays, to visit my parents. And do my laundry. I crack a smile. For the first time in the last few days I'm finally feeling positive about my life. It isn't State, but it's something.

I turn around as I near the end of the path. I figure I've been gone for at least two hours by now. My cell phone is sitting on my bedside table and I don't want Dad to worry, assuming that he has emerged from his room.

Greenville has come to life by the time I pass back through it. It's not as busy as when the film crew was here, that's for sure, but there's a decent number of people out and about. I wonder if the town will ever be the same. It appears normal now, on the surface, but I know everyone, just like Nancy, is still going to be talking about the movie and the crew for years to come. Blegh.

When I get home, Mom's car is still gone and Dad's is in the driveway. I'm glad. I really didn't want to come home and find that he too was gone and the thought had definitely crossed my mind.

I look in the kitchen and in the living room. Dad isn't around. I head upstairs and his door is still closed. My phone chirps as I walk down the hall, so I head into my room and throw my tired body down on the bed and grab my phone. It's a text from Mitch.

Hey, how are you?

What do I even say? I want to be mad at him for being weird and not really paying attention to me at his party. Is it worth it? Did he even notice? I decide to not mention it right now, there's too many other things going on. Like wondering where my mom is….

I'm alright, how are you?

I stifle a yawn as I wait for his reply.

Good. Just started packing a few hours ago.

Right. Of course. I forgot that the football team wanted him there next week. Something about summer practice. My heart sinks. We talked about it a few weeks ago and we had decided he would come back on the weekends, to visit me and his mom, until it was time for me to move into the dorms in the fall.

I don't even want to respond. I feel sad. I just want this all to go away. It won't though, I know that, but a girl can dream.

My phone chirps to signal the arrival of another text from Mitch.

Sorry. I didn't think about that text before I sent it.

It's alright, it's not your fault.

It's not alright, but the second part of my text is the truth. It's my own fault that I didn't get into State.

I hear my dad's door open and then close again and I jump off my bed, tossing my phone on the pillow and I open my door. My dad stops and looks at me. His head is hung and it looks like it's taking everything he has to just shift his eyes to meet mine.

"Dad."

I wrap my arms around him and he starts to cry again. I'm so wrapped up in my own drama that I haven't even paused to think about what he might be feeling and thinking about Mom. He clearly knows something about the whole situation that I don't and so far he hasn't been willing to share it with me.

"Let's go downstairs. We need to talk."

I nod and follow him into the living room. We sit on opposite sides of the couch and turn toward each other. I want to be strong, for him. Tears start to flow from my eyes before he even opens his mouth. I have a pretty good idea of what he's about to say.

"Your mother... she's left *us*... and she isn't coming back."

Based on her odd behavior this week, I could have guessed as much. I just don't think I wanted to admit that to myself.

We sat there in silence. The tension builds to an unbearable point. I close my eyes, take a deep breath, and get ready to say something. He beats me to it.

"She met someone."

I don't even know how to respond to that. My brain is flooded with questions. My parents always seemed happy enough in their marriage, as far as I could tell, so I couldn't even begin to figure out what could have happened. I force myself to not say anything and to just wait for him to continue.

"When I dropped you off at Mitch's, I came home and she was packing."

I'm in shock. This isn't something I would have ever predicted. I'd always imagined that my parents would be happy forever, that they would be that old couple walking down the sidewalk, still holding hands, and that they would be married until the day they died.

"She said she'd send me the divorce papers and that she was never coming back."

I nervously chew on my fingernails.

"Dad, you have to get her back."

He shakes his head. I've never seen him give up on anything before.

"She's gone, Amy."

I don't know whether to try and comfort him or accost him for not even trying to get her back.

"She... she looked me right in the eyes and said 'I

met my soul mate,' and that was it. She didn't seem sorry for what she was doing to our family."

I didn't want to believe it. She had never been so cavalier and now she was just leaving like *that*, without even saying goodbye to me, on the day of my high school graduation.

"Where is she? Who is this guy she ran off with? We need to go over there and bring her home."

His eyes widen. I'm sure I look crazed right now and I don't care. She can't do this to us. I won't let her, even if Dad is defeated, I'll fight for our family. We belong together.

"I'm glad you feel so passionate about it, but we can just go over there."

"Why not?"

I jump up and head for the front door.

"I don't know who he is, she wouldn't tell me, but I know he was a part of the film crew. She let that much slip."

I lean against the door. They had all left. I felt anger course through my veins. She had left us for some Hollywood celebrity and was probably sitting by a pool right now. I pick up a vase, from the table next to the front door, that was given to Mom by her grandma, and I throw it to the floor. Dad looks up, but doesn't say a word.

I run up the stairs to my room, slam my door closed and sit down on the end of my bed. I drop my head as the tears start to flow. There is a soft knock at my door, but I don't get up.

"Honey?"

His voice is muffled, coming through the door.

"If you want to talk, I'm here for you."

I don't respond. I feel bad. He's hurt by her, at least as much as I am, and I'm making this about me and how upset I am at her. I take a few deep breaths and I start to calm down.

What a shitty week.

CHAPTER SIX

It's been a month since she left and when I get home from work, I still expect to see her car in the driveway.

The only thing that carries me through my shitty day as a waitress is that possibility that she will come home, wrap her arms around me and tell me how sorry she was and beg Dad to take her back.

I knew it was never going to happen, but that didn't stop me from imagining every possible way that it could take place. Perhaps the most far-fetched day dream was that she was offered an acting job and that she was going to move us to Hollywood and that we were going to be rich. That would be nice.

Nope. None of that happened. I was constantly disappointed every single day when I came home. Dad, he was still sulking, but seemed like he was trying to make the best of a bad situation. I think his work kept his mind occupied. Mine on the other hand… well it was only a source of income. I had to get out of here, and that wasn't going to happen until I could afford a car.

I don't have anywhere to go really. I guess I could go confront my mom. Tell her how angry I am at her. Beg her to come home. But what good would that do? And then what? Then I would be in Los Angeles. I feel a chill run through my spine at the thought. Something about that place, even though I had never been there, gave me the creeps. If I never set foot in L.A., or California for that matter, that would be just fine.

My legs hurt by the time I get inside. I toss my apron on the coffee table and plop down on the couch. I glance at the clock, it's almost nine. A month ago, I would have been shocked if my dad wasn't home at night. Now he spends most nights, after work, at the bar. I'm usually in my room by the time he gets home.

I push myself off the couch, no easy feat, and head for the kitchen. My feet hurt, not nearly as bad as the first week of my new job. The combination of working eight hour shifts and walking to and from my job has been much more difficult than I ever imagined. I finally understand why adults seem so excited about weekends.

The fridge is empty, like it is most days. I make a mental note to stop at the grocery store on the way home from work tomorrow. I close the door and search the cabinets for something. I find some mac and cheese buried deep, behind some spices and seasonings, and pull it out. A thin layer of dust covers the box. I know it's past the expiration date, so I don't even bother looking at the box for it and I put a pot on the stove, put in the directed amount of water and turn the burner on.

I head upstairs, slowly thanks to the burning sensation in my thighs, and change out of my work uniform. I can say, that if my job has taught me one thing, it's that waiting tables is a hard ass job. After the first week, I promised myself I would always be a good tipper.

I pull my shirt over my head and toss it in the hamper. I hear the front door open and slam close.

"Amy!"

I can hear it in his voice. He's drunk. I finish changing and force myself to stay calm as I walk out of my room into the hallway.

"Amy!"

I freeze at the top of the stairs. I don't know if I want to go down. My hand trembles as I reach for the railing. I've never seen him like this before. This isn't the man who raised me.

"Get your ass down here, right now!"

I turn and run to my room. I slam the door closed and lock it. He climbs the stairs, each thud making my heart beat faster. He is almost to my door. I walk backward, until I reach I bump into the wall. There is only ten feet, and a flimsy door, separating us. I know it isn't enough.

His footsteps grow louder and finally stop. The light from the hall is struggling to peek around his feet. His darkness is swallowing the light. The door handle creaks as he tries to open it. I hold my breath. I know it's locked, but I don't know if that will stop him.

"Open this door!"

I cover my ears as tears start to flow from my eyes. I can't listen to this. He's the only person I have. He can't do this. I slide down the wall and put my head down and try to hum loud enough to drown out his screaming and pounding on the door.

CHAPTER SEVEN

I put my hand up in an attempt to block the sun from hitting me in the eye. It doesn't really do much good. I roll from my back to my side and push myself up. I spent the night on the floor and my body is definitely feeling it.

I'm not sure exactly when my dad stopped pounding on my door, I had my ears covered and I was in a different world by then. I woke up at some point, for just a moment, but the pounding had stopped and I quickly fell back asleep.

The first thought that crosses my mind, when I finally get a grip on standing, is that I should go pound on his door, yell at him and tell him what an asshole he was. I really, really, want to. I know it won't make me feel any better, well… it might in the moment, but I know I'll regret it. That's not who I am, or who I want to be. I'm better than that.

I throw on some comfy clothes and head out into the hall, quietly, and put my ear to Dad's door. I can hear him snoring. He should be up by now, or he'll be late for work, but after last night I'm not waking him up.

Remembering that I have the mid-morning shift at work, I get my clothes ready and set them out and take a shower. After my shower, while I walk down the hall back to my room, I hear a groan come from his room and ignore it. I get dressed quickly, hoping to avoid having to talk to him at all. I still can't believe how he acted last night. I need today, or even more time, to figure out what to say to him.

I head out of the house and start walking to work. I hear my dad calling my name and I ignore him and start to walk faster. After last night, I don't feel the need to even acknowledge him. The mid-morning shift at work hasn't been busy, not since I've been working there at least, so it will give me ample time to figure out what I want to say to him.

Leaving so early for work, and walking fast, gets me there almost an hour early. It's late enough that the morning crowd, which is mostly guys getting ready for a long day of manual labor, has come and gone and the lunch crowd is still a few hours away.

I head inside, with nothing else to do, and take a seat at the bar. Rachel smiles at me and leans against the other side of the counter.

"You're early."

"Yeah… couldn't sleep."

"I can tell. You look like shit," she says.

I'm not sure how to even respond to that.

"Sorry… that didn't come out right. I meant you look tired."

"Can I get some coffee and some scrambled eggs?" I say.

I skipped breakfast, in my haste to get out of the house, and even though the eggs at work are mediocre, I know that I need to eat something or I'll regret it by the time my shift is over.

Rachel nods and smiles. I know that as soon as she turns her back that it will fade. She graduated three years ahead of me, but I was in the same grade as her brother, and so far we aren't getting along. I'm not sure what it is. Ever since I was hired she has been trying to undermine me and make me look bad in front of customers. The few times I asked her to put my orders in for me, they somehow mysteriously were wrong. Something that was blamed on me of course.

She sets the black coffee down in front of me and plops down a milk pitcher with enough force that it spills over the top, just a little. I glare at the back of her head as she turns around to put in my food order.

I put three packets of sugar in my cup and fill it to the top with milk. I bring the cup to my lips and take a sip. I really hope this perks me up some, because it tastes just awful. I don't know what Rachel did to the coffee today, but it's never this bad. I set the cup down and stare at the light brown liquid. I wonder if she maybe did something to my coffee. Would she stoop that low?

Before I can contemplate it any further, she slides my plate of scrambled eggs in front of me and dashes off to greet a customer who has just walked through the door. I take a bite of the eggs and look around while I chew. The eggs aren't very good. I don't have the heart to tell Dylan, the cook who is on shift now, that his food is kind of bad. Maybe it's just me, no one else ever really seems to mind or complain.

The bell on the door rings again as someone else comes in the diner. I turn my head, while chewing my second bite of rubbery eggs, and see that it isn't a customer, but instead it's Lance, the manager. I turn back to my food and wash down the eggs with more coffee.

Lance sits down next to me. I can see him looking at me out of the corner of my eye, so I turn and smile as I swallow only my third bite of eggs.

"You're here early."

Rachel appears and pours Lance a cup of coffee. He takes a sip, sets it down, and turns his attention to her. Thankful for her arrival, I turn back to my breakfast.

"Wow, Rachel, this coffee is fantastic!"

I want to gag. He's such a perv.

"Thanks, Lance, can I get you anything to eat?"

I push my plate away. I don't have an appetite anymore.

"Nah, I'm good. My mom made waffles."

Rachel takes my plate and disappears into the back.

"So, Amy, how's it going?"

I turn my attention, begrudgingly, back to Lance. I want to tell him exactly *how it's going*, but I need my job. Especially after what happened last night. I want to tell him that he's a pig, that he shouldn't hit on his employees and that the only reason he keeps his job is that his parents own the place. I swallow my tongue and tell him what he wants to hear.

"It's great so far. I think I'm really getting the hang of things and Rachel has been super helpful."

His smile is so large that it's making my face hurt.

"That's what I like to hear. She's a great girl, isn't she?"

Lance nods and I follow his line of sight to Rachel. She's leaning forward, at a table of two guys that have just come into the diner, and from what I can tell, she is giving them a pretty generous look down the front of her shirt.

"Yeah… she's *great.*"

If Lance was brighter, I might be worried that he might pick up on my sarcastic tone, but he doesn't even respond. He's much too busy looking at Rachel's ass as she drops her pen and bends over to pick it up. Gross.

It seems so obvious to me that there is something going on between the two of them, and if there isn't there might as well be. Rachel and Lance flirt with each other incessantly, even in front of customers, it's so disturbing.

Lance gets up and heads into the kitchen. I'm still not sure what it is exactly that his parents pay him to do. It seems like a large part of his day is spent eating free food, talking to customers or flirting with Rachel, and when she isn't at work he flirts with pretty much every single female customer.

I don't know what she could possibly see in him. He's gotta be in his late thirties, which isn't old, but he still lives at home and doesn't own a car. It's like he's already reached the peak in his life and he isn't worried that it's all downhill from here. Maybe he doesn't even realize it.

Laughter spills from the kitchen into the dining area. Lance is probably telling Dylan another one of his famous female conquest stories. I walked in on one of them my first week and the graphic description isn't something I'm likely to forget anytime soon. I'm not a prude or anything, but I definitely didn't want to hear that and not coming from Lance, that's for sure.

I spin around in my stool and survey the diner as my last few precious minutes of freedom pass before my shift starts. I see Rachel, back at the table of the creepy guys, and she turns around and points at me. I spin around as quickly as possible, but I can hear crackling coming from their table. My face turns red as I wonder what she could possibly be saying to them.

"Amy!"

I lift my head and see Lance standing at the door to the kitchen, motioning for me. I've never felt so eager to talk to him. I head into the kitchen, where Dylan is cutting onions and has his back turned to us. I turn my attention to Lance.

"Amy, there's something I need to talk to you about."

Oh no. Is he going to fire me? What did I do wrong? I bet it was something Rachel did or said. I'm going to….

"Don't look so scared," he says.

"Huh?"

"You look frightened. Your face just went white."

Lance starts to laugh. Dylan even takes a break

from his onions to turn around and crack a smile at my expense.

"Relax, alright. I'm not going to fire you or anything."

Thank god. I stop holding my breath.

"It's more of a trivial matter, but it was something I wanted to point out to you. It will help keep the customers happy and it will help you make better tips. You want to make the customers happy and make better tips don't you?"

I nod at his stupid question. Of course I do. The more money I make, the faster I can quit this stupid job and move on with the rest of my life.

"Well, Rachel pointed it out initially so I kept a close eye on you for a few days and there's a couple things that you could work on that could take you to another level as a waitress."

I wasn't aware levels of waitressing existed. I knew Rachel had said something. She really needed to mind her own business. I really see no other option other than to play along, at this point at least. I need this job more than any of them know.

"Yeah, I'd be happy to hear what suggestions you might have," I say.

"Great."

He smiles at me and reaches toward me. His fingers wrap around the top button of my work issue polo and pop it open. He reaches for the next, and final button, and I take a step back and glare at him.

"Hey, don't get all excited, I'm just trying to help you."

Of course, he's doing this for my benefit. I'll believe that when hell freezes over. I know that he's got some sort of other motive.

"I'll decide what buttons should stay buttoned."

I leave the shirt slightly more open for now. It's hot in the kitchen anyway.

"Ok… well, have you ever really watched Rachel wait on customers?"

I look out of the kitchen door at Rachel. She is at a table of three male customers who just sat down. She has one hand on her hip and she is chewing on the end of her pen. I don't see what Lance could possibly be wanting me to notice. All I know is that every moment I look at her makes me more angry about having to work with her. Thankfully it's been slow enough lately that we only cross paths and don't have actual shifts together. I duck back into the kitchen and look back to Lance.

"See what I mean?" he says.

"Um… no, I'm not sure what you mean."

"Just think about how she *interacts* with customers compared to you. That's why she makes twice the tips you do."

Is he saying what I think he's saying? It's sounding like he wants me to be flirtatious with the male customers.

"You want me to *flirt* with the customers?"

He looks shocked.

"I never said that."

"But that's what you meant."

Dylan stopped chopping, but still has his back to us, and is listening to the whole conversation.

"No. I never said that. What I'm trying to say, is just try to be a little more *friendly* with the customers, and it will help you and it will help me. They will order more, come more often and you'll make more in tips. We both win that way."

So he wants me to flirt with the male customers. Great. Really great. A chill passes down my spine as I imagine flirting with the vast majority of our male customers. Most of them are old enough to be my dad, or grandpa for that matter. Creepy. The last thing I want to do is get more *friendly* with them, as Lance put it, even if it means increased tips. I'm not that desperate.

"Sure, I'll try that out."

"Good," he says. "I'm sure you'll be pleased with the results."

I just nod. There's no way I'm going to follow his advice, but I need him to think I will. I need this job more than I'm willing to admit.

My shift is about to start, so I grab my apron off the hook in the back, wrap it around my waist and tie the ends behind my back and pull on them to make sure it's snug. I put my order pad in the pocket of the apron and grab a couple of pens. I take a deep breath, put a smile on my face and head into the dining area.

Maybe I'll get lucky and it'll be busy and my shift will just fly by and I'll make some good tips. With my luck though it will be super slow and I won't do well in tips. I just have to keep reminding myself that every dollar I make is a dollar closer to my goal of getting out of here.

In the past few weeks I've begun to refine my plans for the future. I've had plenty of time now that Mom is gone and Dad is spending his days at work and nights at the bar and Mitch is away at school already. I've decided I need to get out of here. I loved this town, at one time, but now… well, there isn't really anything here for me other than my dad and I can always come visit him.

I figure if I can save up enough money, working at the diner, I can move to Salem. That way I can be close to Mitch and I can go to the community college. I need to save up enough to get an apartment and pay for classes and books. Hopefully I can manage that in the next couple of months and that way I can be there for the start of the fall semester.

I figure I've got about six weeks, which unless something changes at work and we get busier, isn't going to be enough time, but I've got to try. Otherwise, I'll be stuck here for at least another semester while I save. I wouldn't have minded that, I mean it's not ideal, but after last night… I just don't know if I want to be around Dad right now, even if he is going through a tough time, I'm not sure if I feel safe. That was the first time I've seen him like that and it scared me.

The bell on the door of the diner goes off and brings me back into reality. I smile at an older couple as they enter and take a booth by one of the windows. I grab a couple of menus and head over to the table.

They greet me with genuine smiles. I do my best to forget about everything that is happening in my life and to focus on them and smile. They are a cute old couple, the kind that every young couple sees and thinks 'hey that'll be us someday' and it makes me miss Mitch.

"Here's a couple of menus for you. Can I get you anything to drink while you look them over?"

"I'll take coffee, black, and a small glass of orange juice for her."

I smile and head off to get their drinks. Rachel and Lance are standing in the far corner of the room, his hand hovering near her side as she smiles and giggles. I'm just glad they are far enough away from the older couple that they won't be heard. I notice the table Rachel had been flirting with is gone. I find it amazing, she doesn't fawn all over Lance when she has a table. She really has flirting with men to get exactly what she wants down. Maybe she isn't as dumb as I think she is, or as dumb as she comes off to other people.

There's a part of me that knows Lance is right in what he told me, but there's no way in hell I would ever stoop to that level, it's just not worth it to me. No matter how much I want to get out of here, it's not worth flirting with old creepy men to maybe get out of here a couple of days sooner, it's not worth a lifetime of memories. Not to me at least. Rachel, on the other hand… I don't think she does it for the money even. I think she does it because she likes the attention from men and she is able to show that she has power over them.

I go back to the old couple's table and set their drinks down and pull out my order pad and a pen. I turn to her first and she smiles.

"Are you ready to order?"

She nods and picks up the menu and pulls it close to her face before setting it down again.

"I'll have the Eggs Benedict with some toast, please."

"White or wheat?"

"White," she says.

I write down her order and turn to her husband. He smiles up at me. They are such a sweet couple.

"Can I get the French toast?"

I nod and write it down. It's an easy order, I didn't really need to write it down, but I've noticed that customers can get nervous if I don't, so most of the time I will just humor people.

"Would you like any bacon or sausage to go with that?"

"Oh no, the French toast will be more than enough for me. When you get to be my age, you don't need that much to eat."

I smile at him. They are so cute together. I head back to the kitchen and give Dylan the order. He smiles as I hand it over and reads it before turning to the stove to start cooking.

Another customer comes into the diner and I turn my attention to them. I feel my heart sink when I see who it is. I didn't expect to see my dad today, especially not at my work, in the middle of the day. I feel anger starting to boil up inside of me. I can't lose my cool, not at work, I know that, but it's going to be a struggle.

His gaze meets mine and I can see on his face that he's not in any position to be in public. My dad's hair is crazy, it's sticking in every direction and he's still wearing his work clothes from the day before. Great.

I storm over to him and before I can say anything I'm nearly knocked over by the overpowering smell of alcohol coming from him. He stinks. He needs a cold shower and a lot of coffee and water and to not be at my work.

"I... I have to talk to you right now," he says.

I shake my head and point at the door. I can't believe he showed up here. I turn around and look toward Lance and Rachel. They are both watching me and my dad.

"Go, now," I say, trying to be quiet so that only he can hear me.

"No, I'm not leaving until you talk to me. You owe me that."

His speech is a little slurred. At first I thought maybe he was just hung over, but now it's obvious that he's been drinking today.

"Get out of here, you're going to get me fired."

I turn to walk away and he grabs my arm and spins me around. Pain shoots through my arm as he squeezes me with his large hand.

"Ow!"

Lance darts across the diner and tries to help me by grabbing my dad's other arm. What Lance doesn't know, unfortunately for him, is that years of working at the mill has kept my dad in peak physical shape. He wraps his hand around Lance's neck, and throws him down. Lance falls into a heap and isn't moving.

While my dad isn't paying attention, I twist free and break out of his hold. I drop to the floor and lift Lance's head. He's breathing, and his eyes are open, but he definitely hit his head and he's going to have quite the headache.

I turn my head and glare at my dad. He spins in a circle, looking at the table with the old couple, who are now cowering in their booth, and Rachel, who is standing behind the counter with a phone in her hand. My dad pauses, as if he's not sure what to do, and without looking at me he runs out of the diner and down the street.

Tears roll down my cheek as I help Lance stand back up. He's uneasy on his feet and almost falls over. He puts his hand on the back of his head and then looks at it to see if he's bleeding. Thankfully he's not.

Rachel sets the phone down and rushes over to check on Lance.

"The police are on their way!"

Great. Just what I need. I knew Dad was about to get exactly what he deserved, given his actions, but that doesn't change the fact that he's my dad and I don't want to lose the only parent I have left.

I don't know what to do. He ran off in the direction of our house. I take off my apron and head for the door.

"Where do you think you're going?"

I turn to face Lance. He looks really angry.

"I'm going to find my dad."

Lance shakes his head.

"That was your dad?"

Well… if I wasn't fired before, I definitely am now.

"Yeah."

"You need to stay here to give a statement to police. I'm going to press charges and they are going to want to talk to anyone who was here during the assault."

"No."

I turn and leave. I don't even wait for him to respond. Lance is going to do whatever he wants anyway. I'm not going to be a part of it. No matter what he does, my dad is the only family I have now and I can't contribute to putting him behind bars for any amount of time.

I pull out my cell and my fingers hover over my dad's number. I know I should call him and warn him that Rachel called the police and that they would be at our house in no time. Instead, I hit Mitch's number and hope that he's not in practice.

The phone rings three times before he picks up.

"Hey, how are you?"

I start to cry.

"What's wrong?"

"I… my dad. He showed up at work and grabbed me and then he threw my boss to the ground."

"Jesus. Are you alright?"

"Yeah, I guess so. I'll probably have a bruise, but I'm OK. I don't know what to do."

"One second."

While I wait, I keep walking in the direction of my house not know what else to do really do. I hear sirens off in the distance. The town is small enough that they are probably heading to the diner right now and then they will be heading to our house shortly.

"OK, I want you to head over to my house. I'll call my mom and tell her you're coming over."

"Should I go home first and tell my dad that the police are coming for him?"

"No, don't go home. I don't trust him to not hurt you."

My dad has never hurt me before, he never even spanked me, but after today I'm not so sure anymore and I think Mitch is right.

"Alright."

"Stay safe, I'll leave as soon as I can. It'll be a few hours until I can get there though."

"Thanks."

I feel a little relieved. It will be good to see Mitch, even given the circumstances.

CHAPTER EIGHT

I knock on the front door of Mitch's house, trying to think of the last time I was actually inside the main part of the house. Even at the graduation party I didn't go inside. The door swings open and his mom, with a sad smile on her face beckons me to come inside.

"Come in, Amy."

"Thanks, Ms. J."

She closes the door and I follow her into the living room. I take a seat on the yellow couch that looks like it's from the seventies, and it feels like it's that old too, and she sits across from me, in a light blue recliner that also looks like it's seen better days.

"So... Mitch told me a little bit about what's happened with you lately."

I just nod as I wonder what he could have possibly told her. I assume that she knows about my mom running off already, seeing as how most of the town knows, but I haven't exactly been telling Mitch everything else that has been going on at home. I have mentioned my dad's drinking to him a couple of times, but that's it, until today.

"Is there anything I can do to help?"

59

"Thank you, but I think I'll be OK."

I'm not sure what she thinks she can do for me. He's my dad and my only family now. Mom made it pretty clear that she didn't want anything to do with either of us when she ran off to Hollywood and didn't leave any way to contact her.

I want to break down and cry. I really do. Things have just been so crappy lately, I feel like nothing is going my way. I just want to run away and never look back.

"Well… if you change your mind, please let me know."

"I will, thanks."

She stands up. I start to stand, too, and she motions for me to stay seated.

"Get comfy, I was just going to make myself so tea, can I get you something?"

"A glass of water would be great, thank you."

"Of course, I bet you're thirsty. Did you have to walk all the way here from work?"

"Yeah, it wasn't too bad, I'm kind of used to it now."

"You poor dear. Stay here and I'll be right back."

She heads into the kitchen and I try to make myself more comfortable on the couch. I try scooting to either side of where I sat down and moving forward and backward. Nothing seems to really help. I give up and instead distract myself by looking around the room. Everything looks like it's been stuck in the early eighties. It's kind of awful.

Ms. J pokes her head back into the room and smiles at me.

"Did you want ice in your water?"

"No, thank you."

She is gone again.

I lean forward and pick up a copy of *Good Housekeeping* from the coffee table and start to flip through it. Nothing really catches my eye and I close it and set it back down. I don't think I'll need to worry about reading something like that for a few years at least.

Ms. J comes back into the living room with a tray and sets it down on the coffee table and takes a seat on the couch next to me. On the tray is a glass of water, a mug with her tea, another mug with what looks like hot chocolate, with little marshmallows floating in it, and a plate of cookies that look homemade. I pick up the glass of water and take a long drink. I set it back down, nearly half empty. I didn't realize how thirsty I actually was. She picks up her tea, pulls the bag out and takes a careful sip in case it's too hot. Apparently satisfied, Ms. J leans back against the couch and turns her attention to me.

"The hot chocolate is for you, Amy, and help yourself to the cookies. They are my mom's recipe. If you don't snag a couple now though, Mitch will come in here like a tornado and eat them all."

She smiles at me as I reach for a cookie and the mug of hot chocolate. I can see the steam rising from it, so I blow on it and decide to eat my cookie while I wait.

There's an explosion of flavor in my mouth and before I know it I'm done with the cookie and already reaching for another.

"I told you they were delicious."

"These are… definitely the best cookies I've ever had."

"I'm glad you like them. If you want, I can show you how to make them sometime."

I smile and nod at her and take a sip of my hot chocolate. It's sweet of her to offer. Even the thought of it reminds me of the fact that my own mom is gone. I hide my emotions behind my mug and hope that she will change the conversation soon.

"So, I hope you don't mind, but I've gotta do a few more chores around here before it gets dark."

"Of course. Do you need some help?"

She stands up, smiles down at me with that

mother gaze of hers and rests her hand on my shoulder.

"No, dear, you take it easy. You can hang out here if you want, or you can go to Mitch's room, it's unlocked."

"Thank you."

Ms. J heads into the kitchen and I hear the door onto the back porch open and close as she heads into the yard. I can't imagine the mental and emotional strength she must possess to keep this farm going by herself.

I finish my hot chocolate and eat another cookie before returning the tray to the kitchen. I wash my water glass and mug and put them in the drying rack and cover the plate of cookies with a piece of foil.

My phone chirps and I pull it out of my pocket. A text from Mitch. I smile, genuinely, for what seems the first time all day.

Be there in an hour. Can't wait to see you.

I let out a sigh as I imagine how nice it is going to feel to have him wrap his arms around me and kiss me.

Drive safe and no more texting. xoxo.

I put my phone back in the pocket of my jeans and head onto the back porch. I head down the steps and go into Mitch's room.

Once the door is closed, I take a deep breath. It smells like him and I instantly feel a little better about my day. I lie down on his bed and close my eyes. Not because I'm tired, but because I feel safe and I want to always feel that.

A few minutes pass before I open my eyes and roll onto my stomach. I notice a journal of some kind sitting on Mitch's bedside table. I pick it up and turn it over in my hands. It's red, with a sort of velvety texture and on the front, in gold letters, it says "Words Are What You Make of Them." I set the journal back down, exactly where I found it. The temptation to read it is pretty strong.

I get up to distract myself from the pull of the journal and walk around the room. Many of the things in the room I was accustomed to seeing are gone now, but it still feels like Mitch. Most of his posters are gone, presumably with him at school and his desk in the back corner is empty. His TV is gone. The couch is still there, too big and heavy to take to school I'm sure. I sit down on it and think back to all the good times we've had on that couch.

Our first kiss came on the couch in his room and so did our last before he left for State. I wonder if we'll ever kiss there again. I mean, I know we will tonight, but past that I don't know. I feel like everything is up in the air right now. I feel uneasy.

I take out my phone and play with it until I hear the door to Mitch's room open. I put my phone away and turn my head just in time to see him walk through the door. He smiles and I jump up and rush toward him. He holds out his arms and lifts me up and spins me around. Mitch sets me down and presses his warm lips against mine and I melt. I didn't realize how much I missed him the last few weeks.

"I missed you," he says.

I can feel my cheeks turning red as he brushes the hair away from my face.

"I missed you, too."

I take his hand and lead him back to the couch and we sit down.

"So… about today…."

"I feel bad that you had to drive all the way back here."

He shrugs and squeezes my hand.

"Anything for you. I can't believe what happened. Are you alright? You seem so calm."

"I'm alright I guess."

Do I really want to tell him everything? I know that I want to, whether or not that's the smartest and best thing to do is a different story. I feel almost like I've already been such a burden on him. I know he's probably tired from football practice and now having to drive all the way back to Greenville to help me.

"Hey," he says, lifting my chin with his hand. "You can tell me anything."

I know I should feel that way and sometimes I really do feel like I can tell him anything… but there are other times… times when I feel like I can't tell anyone what is really going on.

"I know."

He leans forward and kisses my forehead. I can't believe how blessed I am to have such a wonderful and caring boyfriend. Yeah, he has his moments, like at his graduation party, but for the most part he is amazing. We all have our moments.

"What are you going to do?"

I shrug my shoulders. I really have no idea. I feel like I'm floating down a slow moving river, with no idea where it's leading.

"I was kind of hoping that you could help me figure that out," I say.

Mitch strokes his chin with his left hand while he thinks. It's a really cute pose. I wish I was in a better mood and could tease him about it. Just a little.

"Well… you could always run away."

That thought had crossed my mind before, that was for sure. I just didn't know if it was something I could really pull off.

"OK, let's pretend for one minute that I ran away," I say. "Where would I go and what would I do?"

"You don't have to go anywhere… why don't you just move out of your house, when your dad is at work or something, and you can move in here and just stay in my room for now until you save enough to move to Salem."

It was an idea that had actually not crossed my mind.

"I doubt your mom would appreciate me, a seventeen-year-old runaway living in her basement."

Mitch lets out a little chuckle and I do my best to

smile. It was kind of funny, even if it's the truth.

"She wouldn't mind at all. I asked her about it, when I got here and she didn't seem to be opposed to the idea at all."

"Really? I never thought she really liked me very much."

He frowns at me. I deserved that. I have no idea why I just said that. Nothing she has ever said or done should have led to me to believe that. It's my own insecurities and lack of a mother, I think, that is making think that about Ms. J.

"She adores you. She just told me today."

"Well… I guess it's a possibility, but what would I do if I lived here? I can't just hang out in your room all day, alone."

"Just work as much as you can, at the diner, and save your money so that you can move to Salem before the start of the fall semester."

"Yeah… I don't know for sure, but I'm fairly certain that I don't have a job anymore after today."

"Because of what your dad did? I guess that would make sense."

"I kind of also walked out before the police arrived, even though Lance asked me to stay and give a statement."

Mitch cringes.

"I know," I say. "It wasn't the smartest thing to do… but I panicked and I didn't know what to do. It's not like it was something that's happened before."

He wraps his arms around me and pulls me close. His warm touch feels so good. It makes me feel like everything is going to be alright. I know he has my back and that he will protect me.

"I love you," I say.

He kisses the top of my head and moves his lips next to my ear.

"I love you."

A tear, one of happiness, rolls down my cheek and before it can fall, Mitch swipes the tip of his finger across my face and wipes it away.

"Now, don't you worry. We will figure this out."

I nod. I know that we will. I feel like we can do anything and nothing can stop us.

"I think you should move to Salem right now and find a job and go from there. You can't stay in Greenville anymore."

"But I don't have enough money to rent a place, not to mention I'm not eighteen yet. Nobody is going to rent to me."

"Let me worry about that."

"Thank you."

"Now," he says. "Let's go get some dinner, I'm starving. We can just chill out for a little while, watch some TV upstairs and then tomorrow we will figure this all out."

"Don't you have to be at practice tomorrow?"

"Let me worry about all the small details, you just relax and try to forget today."

He takes my hand in his and leads me out of his room and to the main floor. I know he's right. Things are going to work out. We head inside and his mom is already in the kitchen, starting to get dinner ready.

I glance at the clock, it's not quite five. These farmers sure do eat early, I guess it's the whole 'early to bed, early to rise' thing. It's not my cup of tea, but I guess they do what they have to in order to get all their work done.

"Mom, you don't mind if Amy joins us for dinner do you?"

"Of course not, she's always welcome and we always have plenty of food."

While she is talking, I see Mitch out of the corner of my eye shoving two cookies into his mouth and I can't help but smile. She was right about him and the cookies. I guess living in a house of boys means you have to take what you can get.

"Are Shane and Nick going to be here?" Mitch says.

"Shane will be, Nick is over at a friend's house for a sleepover, playing some killing game. Who knows?"

"Did they finish their chores?"

I stand back as Ms. J pulls a meatloaf out of the over before answering her oldest son.

"Yes, they both did. You don't need to worry about them now, I can handle them."

Before Mitch can say anything, and I can tell he desperately wants to make a statement about his younger brothers, the back door opens and Shane walks in.

"Hey, Ma."

He leans in and gives his mom a kiss on the cheek before turning to Mitch.

"What brings you back here, to our little podunk town, bro?"

Mitch lunges forward and puts Shane in a headlock and spins him around so that they are both facing me.

"Amy, I didn't see you there."

"Hey, Shane. How ya been? It's been a while."

"I'm good, just getting ready for football in the fall. I have someone's school records to smash on my way to getting a scholarship at a *good* school."

Shane moves away from Mitch as he finishes his sentence. He knows that if his brother gets a hold of him, he will pay for those jabs, in a brotherly way.

"Hey, go wash up. Both of you."

They both head for the sink. I crack a smile. It's obvious who the real boss of the house is. I can't even imagine that she is able to keep all these boys in check. I look over at Ms. J and I can tell she knows exactly what I'm thinking. She gives me a knowing wink and motions for me to wash up, too.

Mitch sets the table as Shane helps his mom carry

the food into the dining room. I stand to the side, trying not to get in anyone's way and ready to help, just in case they will actually allow me to.

We take our seats at the table, Ms. J at the head of the rectangle, Shane on her right, Mitch on her left and I'm on Mitch's left. The dinner smells really good. I realize the last home cooked meal like this that I had was when Mom was still here.

"Amy?" Ms. J says.

I realize that everyone is staring at me.

"Yeah?"

"I was wondering if you would care to say grace since you are our guest."

It sounds more like a request than a question, so even though I never said grace at my own house I figured as her guest that I could do my best and at least give it a shot.

I follow Mitch's lead and clasp my hands and slightly lower my head.

"Please bless this food and please bless these people. They have seen fit to invite me into their home for this meal and I will be forever thankful for their great generosity."

"Amen," they say, all at once.

I have no idea if that was sufficient or what they were expecting, but everyone is silent as they reach for their forks. Mitch slides his left hand under the table, gives my leg a squeeze and we smile at each other.

The boys are hungry, taking seconds before I get halfway done with my first plate. It's refreshing to see a family that seems so happy. I wonder what it was like when Mitch's dad left. Maybe it was similar to what my dad and I are experiencing right now. Did I not give it enough time? As I look around the table and my eyes settle on Ms. J, I know that the reason the family seems so normal is that she holds it all together.

What am I going to do? Can I really just run off

and leave Dad here, alone? I don't know if I really have a choice.

CHAPTER NINE

Opening my eyes, it takes me a moment to remember where I am and realize why it's so dark. I roll over and look at the clock. Just after eight. I can't believe I slept so late. Usually the sun wakes me up too early. I'm amazed that Mitch was ever able to pull himself out of bed early enough to help with the chores around the farm, I would've slept right through half the day if this was my room.

I sit up in bed and look around the room for him, but he's not around. I turn to the nightstand where I put my phone before I passed out last night. I had set it on top of Mitch's journal. My phone is there, but the journal is gone. I wonder why Mitch would have moved it.

The door to the room opens and my attention is pulled to Mitch, as he walks through. He's carrying a plate of food and a mug.

"I know you're not a big coffee drinker, but I figured we've got a big day ahead of us so you better eat something and get ready."

I smile at him. He's so sweet. Mitch sets the coffee on the nightstand and hands the plate to me and he sits down next to me on the bed.

"Did you eat already?"

"Yeah, I had breakfast with Mom and Shane and helped them with a couple of chores."

I take a bite of scrambled eggs. They are much better than the ones from the diner and I actually don't mind the taste. I follow it up with a bite of toast that has blueberry jam.

"Wow, that jam is amazing!"

"I know right. Mom makes it every year. We have to ration it so that we don't run out before blueberry season rolls around again. It seems like no matter how much she makes, we never have enough."

I smile and take another bite of the toast. I could eat this all day long. Forget eggs, I just want to eat this jam on anything and everything. Heck, I'll settle for a jar and a spoon.

I take a sip of the coffee in an attempt to slow down and make the toast last more than seconds. It's better than the diner too, even black. I take a second sip and set it back down on the nightstand.

"So, how did you sleep?"

I shrug, not really sure how to answer that question. I don't know if I should tell him I slept like crap and I had a night of dreams about both of my parents which left me restless and still tired, especially given how long I slept, or if I should refrain from further burdening Mitch.

"Not too bad, how about you?"

"Somewhere in the middle."

It makes me feel a little better that I'm being sort of honest. I really already feel bad that he's had to come back to Greenville to help me and I don't want to put any more strain on him or our relationship.

He smiles at me and brushes his hand across my arm.

"I slept wonderfully. I had dreams filled with the prettiest lady I know."

I can feel my face turning red. I pick up my coffee and hid my embarrassment by bringing the mug up to my face. He's sweet.

"So," he says. "I was thinking… that once you're done with breakfast, we can head over to your house and pack up whatever you want, drop back the non-essential stuff here and then head to Salem with the rest."

I feel scared. I've felt scared before, heck it's not all that different from what I felt yesterday, but there's something about it that feels… it feels so different and I can't quite put my finger on it. Maybe it's a combination of fear of the unknown and sadness. I feel almost like I'm about to abandon my dad, but I just don't know what to do and now that I've gotten Mitch involved I doubt that there's any way he would let me stay in the same house with my dad for fear of what he might do to me.

"What if my dad's home?"

Am I really going to do this? Run away and start a new life? I guess at this point I don't really have much of a choice.

"I doubt he will be and if he is, let me deal with him."

"Just don't do anything you'll regret."

"Don't worry, I won't do anything stupid. He's smart enough to let you go if I'm there."

I nod. Mitch is probably right and I just need to trust his judgment right now because I'm feeling so unsure about the whole situation. He seems clear about what I should be doing.

"Let's get going," I say.

Mitch takes my plate and coffee mug and takes them to the kitchen while I put my shoes on and I meet him out front, by his truck. We climb in and drive to my house.

It feels like time has slowed on the drive over as I relive all the events from yesterday. I keep thinking about my dad and how he wouldn't let go of me and threw

Lance down. I roll up my shirt sleeve and look at my arm for the first time. I have four bruises on the top of my arm that match where his fingers were. I put my sleeve back down before Mitch can notice. He knows that Dad grabbed me and I don't think he would be so calm if he knew the extent of it.

My dad's car isn't in the driveway when we pull up. Mitch pulls into the driveway across the street and backs his truck toward my garage. Smart. That way we can load up quickly and get out of here as soon as possible. We hop out of the truck and head inside.

The house is in shambles. I've been gone for twenty-four hours and my dad has managed to break pretty much every picture and mirror in the house. Most of the furniture is out of place and one of the dining room chairs is smashed to pieces.

Jesus. There is a pile of beer bottles on the floor in the living room. I shake my head as we go up to my room.

Mitch sits down on my bed while I head to my closet and pull out my two duffel bags. I wish I owned a suitcase, but we never went anywhere that warranted that much stuff. All of our family "vacations" were to places that we could drive to and we typically were only gone for two or three days because of Dad's job. Camping hardly warrants owning a suitcase.

I toss the duffels on the bed and Mitch opens them up and waits for me to start filling them with clothes. In most cases, I would be fairly picky about what I'm packing, but I just want to get out of here as soon as we can. My dad should be at work, but who knows. He could show up at any moment. I shove as many clothes into the first bag and Mitch zips it up while I start to pack the second one.

Even though I know we need to hurry, I take a deep breath and sift through some of the stuff on my desk and my bookshelf. There are a few things that I want to keep still. A photo album of me and Mitch that he made for me on our first anniversary and my yearbook from this year. Other than that, everything in my room suddenly seems like it doesn't have any meaning.

Hanging from a nail in the wall next to my bed is my necklace. I haven't worn it since Mom left and even looking at it right now brings back memories that I'm not ready for. Part of me wants to just leave it, and there is still some part of me that is saying that I need to take it. I pull it off the nail and shove it into my pocket. It isn't valuable or anything, but she gave it to me on my tenth birthday and I have worn it every day since... until the day she left.

Mitch waits in my room while I grab my toiletries out of the bathroom and shove them in a grocery bag and go back into my room. Mitch is standing next to my dresser and in his hand is a framed picture. He sets it back down, when he realizes I'm in the room and lifts the duffel bags off the bed.

"You ready?"

I shrug. I'm as ready as I'll ever be. He walks by me and out of the room. I stay behind and pick up the picture he was just looking at. It's a picture from a couple of years ago, maybe two, and it's of me and my parents. We all looked so happy. Life was so much easier then. At least that's what I thought. Who knows what it was really like. I put the photo down and walk out of the room.

Mitch is waiting for me downstairs with the bags.

"You should write your dad a note, telling him that you're leaving."

"Really?"

"Yeah, I think you should. Just so that he knows why you left and that you aren't coming back and so that he at least knows that you are safe. He may be an ass, but he's still your dad."

Fair enough. I nod and head into the kitchen to find a pad of paper and a pen.

"I'll be in the truck. Take your time and say everything you need."

I lean against the kitchen counter as Mitch walks out the back door. I don't really know what to write. I haven't given it any thought, I was sort of planning on just leaving and I thought that would be the end of it. Mitch is right though, if I did that my dad might worry and report me as a runaway or try to come after me. He still might do that, but it's worth a shot.

Dad,

I can't do this anymore. I'm leaving today and I'm not coming back. After yesterday I just didn't know what to do. I think it would be best for me to move on. There's nothing left for me here, anyway. I hope that you understand. It's not your fault, and it's not my fault that Mom left and there's nothing that either of us can do now, she's gone and never coming back. Please take care of yourself, Dad. You're a good man, don't forget who you are. Don't lose yourself.

Love Always,

Amy.

Tears flow freely from my eyes as I sign the note. It's almost hard to believe that this is happening. I set the pen down, take one last look around the house that I have called home for my entire life and head out the back door. I dry my tears and climb into the already running pickup.

He pulls into the street and in the side mirror I watch as my house fades into the distance. There's a feeling deep inside me that it won't be the last time I'm there. I push the feeling out of my mind and just think about right now and what I'm going to do. I'm about to start the rest of my life and I'm scared. I look over at Mitch. He has a content and calm look on his face.

It makes me feel a little easier as we pass through Greenville, headed toward the rest of our lives, together.

CHAPTER Ten Once we are clear of Greenville, I feel like I can finally breathe again. It's almost like a huge weight has been lifted. I know it's going to be hard, but I can already feel this was a good decision and everything will work out in the long run. It always does.

"So… I was thinking that until you get a job and a place of your own you could stay with me."

"In the dorms?"

Mitch lets out a short chuckle.

"No, the dorms don't open until the week before school. Right now I'm staying in off campus housing that is rented out to football players before the start of the school year. It isn't glamorous, but it works."

"I can't complain, I'll get to be with you."

"Just be prepared to be surrounded by a bunch of sweaty, stinky, guys all day. It's not that fun, trust me."

He's right. It doesn't really sound like my cup of tea, but I don't have any other option, so I'm sure that it will work out just fine.

"I'm sure it will be fine, I can deal with you, I can deal with any amount of stinky, sweaty, football players."

I give Mitch a playful slug in the arm and he cracks a smile.

"Did I do the right thing?" I say.

"Yeah. I don't know what else you could have

done. Your dad didn't leave you with much of a choice."

I'm not sure why there's a feeling of doubt in my mind, for what I did and for what Mitch is saying. I can't explain it. I push the thought out of my mind, I know that now is not the time to question the biggest decision of my life. I can't worry about whether or not it was right or how it's going to turn out. Only time will tell.

When we get to Salem and pull up in front of the campus housing, just after noon, I can tell that Mitch wasn't kidding. This was not what I was expecting, not even after what he told me. The building looks run down and I can't believe the school chose this place for the football players to live. Surely they could afford something nicer with all the money they charge for tuition and the money that the football team brings in every year.

Mitch pulls into an empty spot near the front of the building, turns off the truck and looks over at me, with a smile on his face.

"You ready?"

"I guess?"

He laughs and climbs out of the truck. I take my bag of toiletries and my purse and Mitch gets the two duffel bags out of the bed. I wait for him to take the lead and I follow him inside.

His room isn't too far down the main hall, just the third door on the right, which is nice. He sets down one of my bags, unlocks the door and we go in.

Mitch turns around to gauge my reaction and he starts laughing instantly. I didn't think I was that easy to read.

"That bad?" he says.

"No… it's… it's cozy."

A generous description, that's for sure. The room is tiny, maybe ten by ten and there are two single beds, one against each of the side walls and a small window, with no curtains, that faces the parking lot.

There is a small table under the window that has a

lamp, whose shade has seen better days, which appears to be the only light in the room. I look behind the door, expecting to find a tiny bathroom, but it's just a wall.

"Where's the…."

"The bathroom?"

"Yeah."

I look behind the door a second time, as if the bathroom was going to suddenly appear. Mitch sets my duffel bags on the right bed and sit down on the other bed.

"I forgot to tell you about that. There's no bathrooms in the rooms. The closest one is about forty feet down the hall, on the right."

I take a deep breath. OK… I can do this. Don't panic, Amy, it's going to be like going to camp. I never went to camp, but still the basic concept of what I've seen on TV and in movies should apply. I guess it shouldn't be too bad actually, it's all football players here, so I should have a bathroom all to myself.

"I have to pee, I'll be right back."

"I'll be here."

I set my bag and purse down on the bed and head into the hallway and go right. After what I would guess is about forty feet, I turn to the right and push the door to the bathroom open, without thinking.

"Whoa!"

I look up and see a guy, wrapped in only a towel standing just a few feet in front of me. He's perfect. His wet blonde hair is spread enough so that he can see me and he flashes me a beautiful smile. I spin around and rush out of the bathroom as my face begins to turn the color of a beet. I look across the hall, but the door is just for another room and not a bathroom. I go further down the hall, looking over my shoulder the whole time, hoping that that guy doesn't come out.

I reach the end of the hall, which is only about another fifty or sixty feet and there isn't another bathroom.

Weird. I head back toward the first bathroom and go past it, picking up my pace a little and walk down the other hall.

This time, when I find the bathroom, I look at the door first. I pause and frown. This one says that it's the Men's' room. I'm confused. Did I go into the right one the first time and it was the guy who wasn't supposed to be in there. That's the only explanation.

"You lost?"

I turn around and I'm face to face with the toweled man that I had walked in on. He smiles and I look down. Yeah, he's got a towel on, but it's only covering his bottom half and the top of it is low enough that it doesn't leave much to the imagination.

"I… I…."

He laughs and then walks off, clearly aware that I'm too embarrassed to speak. I want to look over my shoulder and catch one last glimpse of him. I know better than that. What harm did looking ever do though? I turn my head just enough to get a glimpse of him standing only ten feet away. In the process of opening the door to his room our eyes meet. I turn and practically run back to Mitch's room. Stupid. I shouldn't have done that.

I close the door behind me and lean against it. I still have to pee. I can't just leave now though, Mitch will obviously know that something is up.

"Did you get lost or something?"

"Yeah… actually I couldn't find the Women's room. I found two bathrooms and they were both Men's."

"Oh, yeah… sorry about that. I forgot that there's only Men's rooms in this building since it's for football players."

"What?"

"You seem so surprised."

"Well, where are the girls supposed to pee?"

"There aren't any girls that stay here. There's an identical building just down the street for the female athletes to stay in before the start of school."

Emma Keene

Crazy. I wish he would have mentioned this earlier. Where the heck am I supposed to go to the bathroom? And shower for that matter? I was already trying to prepare myself to have to shower and use a bathroom that was more like what you would find in a dorm or locker room, but this... this was just something different altogether.

"What am I supposed to do?"

"Just use the Men's' room. It's not that big of a deal."

"It is a big deal! I can't just walk into a Men's' room. What if there's a naked guy in there or something?"

"OK, fine. I'll tell you what. I'll go with you, make sure that there's no one in the bathroom and then I'll stand guard at the door while you go, and make sure that no one comes in."

We leave his room and head down the hall to the bathroom I walked into and Mitch sticks his head in and looks around.

"Hello? Is there anyone in here?"

He waits for a response but none comes after twenty seconds. He steps aside and holds the door open for me. I walk in, and even though he's already looked, I glance around the bathroom to make sure it's empty before I head for the closest stall.

After what I'm sure is the quickest start to finish pee of my entire life, I quickly wash my hands and open the door. Mitch has his back to me, watching both directions to make sure no one has tried to come in.

"Can I come out?"

He turns around and smiles at me, doing his best to not laugh.

"Yeah, it's safe. No one walked by or tried to come in."

There is a certain amusement in his voice. I can tell that he wants to tease me about it and is doing his best to hold off. We walk back to his room and he walks in first.

"Dude!"

Mitch walks over to a guy who is sitting on the bed on the left side of the room, the one that I had sat on and assumed was going to be mine.

"What's up?"

Both oblivious to my existence, I close the door and just wait.

"You missed a killer practice this morning, dude. Where were you?"

"I was… oh right," Mitch says, turning around and pointing at me. "This is Amy, my girlfriend. This is Spencer. I had to go pick her up from Greenville yesterday and we just got in."

"Hey, Amy, how's it goin?"

"Fine."

I guess maybe these guys go to their friends' rooms and hang out when they aren't practicing. It's a little weird to me, but I get it. Hopefully he will leave soon. I want to spend some alone time with Mitch, I feel like we've just been rushing around, trying to get me out of Greenville.

Spencer sprawls out on the bed and puts his head on the pillow and his arms behind his head to prop it up. Mitch sits on the other bed and they continue to talk. There's not even a chair in this room. I guess I'm stuck standing.

"Did you clear that with Coach?"

Mitch shakes his head. I assumed he had gotten permission to come and get me. Now I feel even worse. I really hope that he doesn't get into trouble with his coach, especially since he's a freshman and trying to make a good impression.

"Seriously?" Spencer says, sitting up on the bed.

"I didn't have time, dude. It's fine, I'll go talk to him later and work it out."

"It's your ass. You should go to his office before

afternoon practice though, or he's going to make you run wind sprints."

Mitch lets out a groan. I've never done a wind sprint, but I can tell by the name and his reaction that he definitely doesn't want to do them.

"What time is it?" Mitch says.

I pull out my cell phone to check the time for him and notice that I've got three missed calls and five text messages, all from my dad.

"It's five after one."

They both jump up and look at me like I'm blocking the door. I step deeper into the room, close to the window and they go toward the door. Spencer leaves and Mitch stops and turns around.

"Sorry, Baby, I forgot that we have a freshman meeting, at one. I'll see you tonight, after practice."

I motion for him to go. I know that leaving yesterday to come get me could be detrimental to his position on the team, so I can't even ask him to explain. I sit down on the bed and look at my phone again as he closes the door, leaving me alone in the room.

I look out the window and can see them running to his truck and speeding out of the parking lot. Hopefully they don't get in trouble for being a little late.

It feels good to be here. Well, not here exactly… this place is a little weird, but it feels good to know that I will get to see Mitch tonight.

I pull out my phone. I have nothing else to do really and I have no idea how late Mitch is going to be. The text messages and voicemails from my dad are sitting there. I really don't feel like I can open them yet. What good could possibly come from reading them?

It's a nice day out, so I might as well go for a walk and get some fresh air and explore the area a little, seeing that I live here now. I lock the door behind me, since Mitch has the only key and I don't want my stuff just sitting in the unlocked room, and I head out through the front door.

The road that we drove down to get here is to my right, so I turn to the left and start walking down the sidewalk. I walk slowly, looking at the buildings that line the street. There a few fraternities and sororities, with large Greek letters hanging above the front door, but I don't recognize most of them.

The street is fairly quiet, with only a car or two passing every couple of minutes as I walk. I have a feeling that once school starts it will be a different story.

After a few more minutes, I come to another street, one that is four lanes total instead of the two lane road I've been walking along, so I go left. I'm starting to get hungry and since I have no idea when Mitch is going to be done with football, I might as well get a snack or something to hold me over until dinner.

There are a few stores and three bars within the first few blocks. I cross over another road, College Ave., and go into the first little restaurant I see. I've never heard of it, Burgers-R-Us, so it must be a local place and not a chain. I see the sign just inside that says 'Seat Yourself' so I sit down at a booth by the window and start to scan the paper menu that's already on the table.

True to their name, their menu is mostly burgers, which sounds a little heavy for what I want. I decide on a chicken Caesar salad and set my menu down while I wait for the waitress to make her way over to me.

"What do you want?"

She blows a big, pink, bubble and lets it pop as she stands in front of me with her order pad. Nice.

"Chicken Caesar, please."

"And to drink?"

She smacks her lips as she chews the gum and starts to blow another bubble.

"Water."

She nods and walks away. I wonder if she noticed the mortified look on my face. I'm no expert waitress, by any means, but even in the month I spent working at the diner, I would never wait on a table while chewing gum. It's just so tacky.

I look out the window, partly to distract myself from watching the irritating waitress and she mills around the near empty restaurant, but mostly because I want to people watch. It's very different and more fun than sitting along Main Street in Greenville, there's never much to see.

A couple walks by the window, holding hands, and they each have a Chihuahua on leash. I almost laugh out loud. They are dressed just like their dogs. He is wearing a blue sweater, has a blue leash in his hand and his dog is wearing a blue sweater, too. The woman and her dog are dressed in the same way, but they are wearing pink. It's kind of cute and silly.

I turn my attention to my waitress as she sets down my water and I smile at her. She doesn't notice and walks away. I shrug. Whatever, she's weird, that's not my fault.

An ambulance, with its siren wailing drives by, dodging cars that are quickly pulling over to get out of its way. I watch it until it disappears and the siren fades. I wonder where they are headed. That's definitely not a sight, or sound, that I'm accustomed to. Now that I think of it, it's really noisy here, especially compared to Greenville. That's going to take some getting used to. I wonder if I'll be able to sleep at night.

The waitress returns, drops off my salad and walks away. I take a sip of the water and almost spit it out. It leaves a funky taste in my mouth. I wonder if there's some soap residue or something in the glass. I try to get the waitress' attention, but she's standing at the table of what looks to be a group of college students. I give up as she sits down at the table with them, her back to me. Whatever.

I look around the table, noticing that I don't have a napkin or any silverware. I let out a sigh, glance in the direction of my waitress and grab what I need from the next table over. I wonder where her manager is, because if it was me, I would fire her. I've never seen such bad service in my life.

The salad isn't bad, not like the water, but it's definitely not the best salad I've ever had. I guess I would say that it's better than most of the food that they served at the diner, especially when Dylan was cooking. I put some salt and pepper on it and it improves the taste and blocks out the slight taste of anchovy from the Caesar dressing.

Once I'm done eating my salad I push it away from myself and look for the waitress. I'm ready to get out of here and see what else is in the area. She's not around, and the table she was sitting at earlier is now empty.

I look around the restaurant and notice I'm alone in here and head toward the kitchen.

"Hello?"

I hear whispering coming from the kitchen, so I move a step closer and call out again.

"Hello?"

The waitress comes out of the kitchen, her lipstick smeared around a bit and she looks embarrassed. I wonder if she forgot that I was there.

"Yes?"

"I'm ready for my check."

She heads over to the cash register, looking over her shoulder toward the kitchen as she walks. I glance that way too, and spot another one of the employees before he can duck back into the kitchen. He's not quick enough and I notice some red residue on his cheek and lips. I hold back a laugh and turn my attention back to the waitress, who is still trying to figure out how much I owe her.

"Six dollars and forty-seven cents."

She hands me the bill, which I glance at, and I set my purse on the counter, take out my wallet and hand her a ten. I leave her a dollar, which more than she deserves, and ignore the scowl on her face as I put the rest of the change in my wallet and leave.

This is going to have to be a one-time treat, I can't afford to keep eating out, if I'm going to get my own place anytime soon. I have a few hundred dollars saved up from working at the diner and it's going to have to last me. What I really need is to find a new job, somewhere close that I can walk to. Plus, that would give me something to do during the day while Mitch is at football.

It's still going to be a few hours until Mitch is done with practice, so I head down the street further and see if there's any places where I might be able to find a job. There's a few places, all places that I had never heard of before that looked like they catered to students. None of them had a help wanted sign in the window and a few of them even had signs saying that they were not hiring. I guess getting a job, especially a waitressing job, in a college town is going to be a little more difficult than I thought.

Feeling a little discouraged, I turn around and head back. I peek at my phone and see that it's only three o'clock. Ugh. I guess I should have asked Mitch for the room key, I just wasn't thinking about it at the time.

CHAPTER ELEVEN

When I get back, which takes less time since I wasn't scouting out the area, I sit on the front step of the building and pull out my phone. I know I'm going to have to check my texts and voicemails at some point, so since I have the time I should just do it now. I take a deep breath and start to read the first one, which is from last night.

Amy, please call me when you can. We need to talk. Dad.

OK, that's not too bad. The next one is from an hour later.

Please answer your phone.

He seems a little irritated, but not angry. At least he said please. The third text is from twenty minutes later.

Answer your phone.

The fourth is dated seven minutes after the previous one. I can tell that he's getting increasingly agitated with each one that goes unanswered.

Amy, don't ignore me, I know you have your phone.

His fifth, and final text is the only one from today.

Don't do this. Don't throw your life away like this. Mitch isn't worth it.

I never should have showed him how to text. I shake my head and try to keep myself from crying. Does he really not get it? I'm not sure what else I could have done or said in my note to make it more clear to him. And why would he think this is about Mitch? Even if I weren't with Mitch, I would have still found a way to get away from Greenville. It might not have been as quick, but I couldn't stay there much longer.

A tear slides down my cheek and drops onto the screen of my phone. I wipe the tear away with my finger and put my phone in my purse. I can't imagine hearing his voice, especially after reading his texts, so I will have to wait to listen to the voicemails. I put my head in my hands and take a deep breath.

"Is everything OK?"

The voice sounds familiar, but in my current state I can't quite place it. I drop my hands and turn my head. Sitting next to me, on my left, is the toweled man from the bathroom. He smiles at me as my eyes grow wider.

"You don't say much, do you?"

I nod. I have no idea what to say and that's not how I would ever describe myself, but I still feel embarrassed about barging in on him earlier. I stand up and turn toward the door. He puts his hand on my shoulder and I stop. A feeling of calm passes through my body. Normally I would want to get away, I don't know him, but there's something about him… something I can't quite put my finger on, that makes me feel better. Thoughts of my dad, my mom, and my life in Greenville vanish from my mind as I turn and look into his emerald green eyes.

"Hi," he says, after I stand, staring at him, for a good thirty seconds.

I can feel my cheeks turning red, so I lower my head a little in hopes that he doesn't notice. He drops his hand from my shoulder and I glance up at him.

"Hi."

"Are you doing alright? You look sad."

I nod. Does he even really care? I still have no

idea who he is or what he's doing here. I assumed that only football players lived in this building and that they were all at practice still.

"Yeah, I'm fine."

I feel a twinge of guilt for lying to him, which is strange considering I just met him and will probably never see him again.

"Really? You don't look fine, but if you don't want to talk about it, it's cool. I get it."

The thought of telling him what's wrong actually does cross my mind, not that he would care or feel any sort of compassion for me. I can't explain why, it just seems like if I was going to tell anyone what's wrong, he would be the person who would understand me. It's a weird feeling and it's making me a little uneasy.

"Thanks for the offer."

I decide to keep it to myself. He doesn't need to be burdened with my life problems. He shrugs, turns and starts to walk toward the parking lot. He stops, taps his left foot and turns around and smiles at me.

"Hey, I was just going to go grab a bite to eat. You should come with me."

No. I'm not going to get into a car with a guy I just met. Plus, I just ate.

"Sure."

Why did I just agree to that? Before I realize what's happening, I'm clicking my seatbelt on, in his brand new SUV, and he is driving out of the parking lot. It's almost like I have no control over my body and it's making decisions for me.

"I'm Logan, by the way."

"Amy."

"Nice to meet you."

He holds out his hand and when I shake it, the same calming feeling passes through my body again. There's something about this boy.

While he drives, I try to not look at him. My eyes

keep drifting in his direction, but his focus is on the road enough that I don't think he notices. He glances over at me and I turn my head to the right and look out the window.

Logan slows the SUV and pulls into the parking lot of a restaurant I've never heard of before. He parks and jumps out and before I can even get my seatbelt off he's made his way to my door and is holding it open for me. He holds out his hand to help me out.

"I'm good, thanks."

I hop down and he closes the door. I think that for a brief second a frown crossed his face when I didn't let him help me down, but I can't be sure.

Logan hurries ahead of me and opens the door. I smile at him and head inside. We stand in line, waiting to be seated, in silence. I'm starting to feel a little weird about the whole situation. I have no idea why I agreed to go with him. He seems like a nice guy though and I don't want to be rude. Not to mention I have no idea where we are.

The line moves forward slowly and we are eventually sat at our table by an overly happy girl. We sit and I do my best to look at the menu and not pay attention to Logan. I feel like every time I even glance in his direction he is looking at me. Not in a bad way, or anything, but it's making me blush.

"What are you getting?" Logan says.

"Uh… I'm not really that hungry."

He raises his left eyebrow and just looks at me.

"What?" I say.

"Oh, nothing. Just humor me and order something. I'll feel bad otherwise."

I scan the menu, trying to find something cheap that I can order. I really need to be careful about spending money.

"You don't even have to eat it, I just can't sit here and eat while you sit there."

I set the menu down as our server comes with

water and pulls out his order pad.

"What can I get ya?"

Logan looks at me and waits for me to order.

"Can I get the side of fruit please?"

"Sure, and for you, sir?"

"I'll have a cheeseburger, medium rare with cheddar, a side of fries and a chocolate milkshake."

"Wonderful, do you need anything else?"

"Yeah, she doesn't want the fruit, she'll take the same as me."

The waiter nods and writes it down on his pad and is gone before I can open my mouth to protest.

"I... I'm really not hungry."

I start to stand, I can't afford to order that much, not to mention I'll never be able to eat it all. Logan puts his hand on mine and looks into my eyes. I sit back down.

"You've never been here, just trust me, you'll want to eat it all. And if you can't no big deal, just take it to go. Plus, I'm paying, you can't turn down a free meal, that's just rude."

His tone is playful and he smiles at me and I can't say no. I'm not going to let him pay for me though, that would just be... a little awkward. He must know that I have a boyfriend though, right? Why else would I have been at the football player's summer house?

"How do you know that I've never been here before?"

"Because, I've never seen you before and I know everyone at school. Everyone worth knowing at least."

Even though what he's saying sounds kind of egotistical, there's something in the way he says it that makes him sound so convincing.

"I'm not in college."

He raises his eyebrow and looks at me as if he's trying to decide if I'm telling the truth. I mean, technically I am, I don't go to school with him. I don't really feel like telling my life story to a guy I just met.

"Logan!"

We both turn and see a guy wearing a State football jersey, with a big blue number eight on the front, and Logan waves to him. The guy points at Logan and turns to the woman he's with. She seems uninterested and keeps walking toward the front door.

"Who is that?" I say.

"I have no idea."

"I thought you said you know everyone at school?"

"Everyone worth knowing."

"Isn't he on the team though? He was wearing a football jersey."

Logan just cracks a smile. Our server sets down our chocolate milkshakes. I'm not sure what to think. He seems so confident and full of himself, but it somehow works and he still comes across as being a nice guy.

I take the straw of the milkshake in my mouth and take a sip. It's so thick that I can barely get any. I look up at Logan, who is grinning at me as he spoons the thick chocolate into his mouth. I pick up my spoon and follow his example. It's really too thick to be a shake, I think, but it tastes amazing. I wasn't really feeling hungry, not after my salad for lunch, but I'm managing to eat it more quickly than Logan is.

I finally take a break from the chocolaty goodness and set my spoon down. Logan has already stopped, only eating about a quarter of his. I look down at mine. I'm mortified when I notice that half of it is already gone.

"It's good, huh?"

"Very."

"I mean, I wouldn't really call it a chocolate shake, it's pretty thick," he says, "but that's what they call it, so who am I to argue?"

I want to tell him that I was thinking the same thing, but I decide that it might sound a little weird and like I'm trying to flirt with him. That's the last thing I want him to think.

Our waiter comes back, this time with our burgers and fries and sets them down before I can open my mouth and say something stupid. Hopefully this will distract Logan enough that he won't ask me any questions about who I am or what I'm doing here if I'm not a student.

He picks up his burger, lifts it to his mouth and pauses. I quickly take a bite of mine to avoid having to answer a potential question.

"Do you go to community college?"

I shake my head and swallow the bite of hamburger. Holy crap, it's really freaking good. This food is so much better than the diner.

"I'll figure it out if I have to keep asking you all night."

Jesus. There's something about him that I actually wouldn't mind that. I push the thoughts out of my mind and focus on Mitch. Mitch. I wonder what he's doing right now. He must be at practice.

"What?" Logan says.

"I didn't say anything."

"No, but you were frowning. Is something wrong?"

"Oh, no, everything is fine. I was just wondering why you aren't at football practice."

For the first time since meeting him, the happy look fades from Logan's face and he sets down his burger. He doesn't look sad exactly, it's more of a look of disappointment.

"I… I don't really want to talk about it if you don't mind."

"Sorry, I didn't…."

Logan waves his hand at me and takes another bite of his burger.

"Don't worry about it, let's talk about something a little less… serious."

I grab the ketchup bottle and squirt some out

onto my fries and hand the bottle to Logan who does the same. I eat three of them and wait for Logan to say something. I wasn't sure what he wanted to talk about, but it clearly wasn't football.

"How is everything?"

Our server showing up distracts us from each other, both of us really not knowing what to say.

"Great," Logan says.

I nod to show my agreement. It actually was. I know it's not the best food in the world, but it's definitely the best burger, fries and milkshake I've ever had.

"So, do you have a boyfriend?" Logan says, finally breaking the long awkward silence that has lasted the last few minutes.

It finally dawns on me that maybe Logan isn't just a nice guy. Maybe he thought this was something more than I did. I thought he was just trying to be friendly. He must have some sort of other intentions for taking me out to eat. Crap.

"I've gotta pee, I'll be right back."

I jump up from the table and head toward the back of the restaurant, hoping that I was heading in the right direction. I see the sign for the bathroom and push open the door to the women's, head into the first stall and sit down.

Stupid. Stupid. Stupid.

What are you doing? You shouldn't be here. What if Mitch comes back from practice and you aren't there and he see's you coming back with Logan? I can't ruin what I have with Mitch because of Logan, it's not worth it and I don't even know him. They probably know each other. I'm so mad at myself. What was I thinking?

I've gotta get out of here, right now. I can't even face Logan. I'm too embarrassed. I'm gonna have to find my way back.

I stick my head out of the bathroom, glance toward Logan and see that he's got his phone out and isn't looking my way. I duck out of the bathroom and head toward the back of the restaurant. The only thing back there is a service station and an entrance into the dishwashing area.

"Do you need something?"

I spin around. There's a server from the restaurant, standing with a hand on her hip. I know that she probably thinks that I'm up to something. She's definitely not happy with me standing in a part of the restaurant that I shouldn't be in.

"I… um…."

I tilt my head and glance over her shoulder. She follows my gaze and when she looks at me again she's smiling.

"Bad date?"

I just nod.

"I get it. Go through here," she points to the entrance to the dishwashing station, "and head through the door at the back of the room. You'll end up in the alley."

"Thanks."

She turns and leaves and one last glance at Logan confirms that he's still occupied. I feel a twinge of guilt. He didn't do anything wrong, not really. I should have told him I couldn't go get something to eat and that I had a boyfriend. That's my fault. I'm an idiot. He doesn't deserve this. I don't see any other way though. I go through the dishwashing station, drawing confused looks from the two guys working there, and head out the back door.

I let out a deep sigh of relief once I'm outside and the door closes behind me. I feel better. I better get back, I have no idea how long it will take and I need to be back there before Mitch is done with practice.

~~~~

When I finally get back, I walk through the parking lot but don't see Mitch's truck or Logan's SUV. I sit down and catch my breath. I practically ran most of the way back, glad that it was pretty much a straight shot from the restaurant and I didn't have a chance to get lost.

The sun is dropping behind the buildings when Mitch pulls into the parking lot and hops out of his truck. He walks over to me, lifts me off my feet and kisses me. My whole body tingles as our tongues touch. He sets me down and gives me a peck on the cheek.

"I missed you."

"I missed you, too," he says.

He takes my hand and leads me inside. We go into his room and we sit on his bed.

"How was practice?"

He shrugs. I can tell by the sweat dripping down the side of his face that it was hard.

"Alright I guess. How was your afternoon? Did you get bored of sitting here?"

"Yeah… I actually went for a walk and tried to find some places nearby that were hiring."

"Any luck?"

He stands up and pulls his shirt off over his head. I stare shamelessly at him as he picks up his towel and shower kit. My thoughts drift to Logan, standing in the bathroom in just a towel and I quickly push it out of my mind.

"Not really."

"You'll find something. I'm gonna go grab a quick shower and then we can get some food."

I watch him leave and then lie down on the bed. I wonder why I thought about Logan. It's kind of weird and not like me. Before I can make myself feel any worse, the door to the room opens and I sit up, expecting it to be Mitch, but instead his friend, Spencer, walks into the room and sits on the other bed.

"Hey, Amy, how's it goin?"

"Good. Mitch is showering."

"OK...."

Spencer stands up, kicks his shoes off and pushes them under the bed and grabs a towel off the rack and leaves the room.

It finally dawns on me. I don't know why it took me so long, but Spencer isn't just a friend of Mitch's... they are roommates and the other bed in the room isn't for me, it's Spencer's. Well, where the heck am I going to sleep?

Eyeing the floor pushing my foot into the commercial carpet, I cringe at the complete lack of give. I sure hope it's not on the floor. Maybe Mitch can find an extra cot or something for me to use. That must be it, because Mitch seemed fairly confident that me sleeping here wasn't a big deal.

It's only about five minutes before Mitch comes back into the room, with the towel wrapped around his waist and his shorts, socks and shoes in one hand and his shower kit in the other.

He tosses the dirty clothes into a pile in the corner and takes the towel off and hangs it up. I close my eyes and look away.

"Seriously?" he says.

"What?"

"You closed your eyes? It's not that big of a deal."

"It is, kind of."

"It's not."

"I want my first time, our first time, to be special. I don't want it to be in *this* room, right now. Not with everything that's been going on."

He lets out a sigh. I feel kind of bad. Most of my friends in high school had sex with their boyfriends on a regular basis and I felt kind of bad for not doing it with Mitch, but I want it to be perfect and I'm not going to do it until I'm certain that I'm not going to regret doing it too soon.

Before we can launch into a full argument over it, and it wouldn't be the first time, the door to the room opens again and Spencer walks in. I pull out my phone and look away as he changes.

"It's safe," Mitch says.

I put my phone in my pocket, remembering that I still haven't listened to the three voicemails from my dad. I know that I'm going to need to be in a good space before I do.

"So… where am I supposed to sleep? Can we get a cot or something?"

Spencer sits down on his bed and pulls out his phone. It's awkward to have a third person, especially one that I don't know, in the room.

"We're going to have to share my bed," Mitch says.

This should be interesting. The bed is small, I guess I would call it a single and I wouldn't like to sleep in it for any length of time by myself, and now I'm sharing it with Mitch, who is definitely not a small guy.

Yay….

"Maybe tomorrow we can start looking for a place for me to live."

I feel like I'm going to need to pee soon, like within the next few minutes. I don't know how long I can keep this up. I need a place of my own, somewhere where I can actually go to the bathroom without Mitch standing guard and I have my own bed. I guess I should be thankful though, Mitch didn't have to rescue me and he did. I really shouldn't complain, I have missed him terribly since he left Greenville.

I smile at Mitch and mentally prepare myself for a night of sleeping on my side, crammed into this tiny bed with Mitch, and take a deep breath. Tomorrow is a new day.

CHAPTER TWELVE

To say that I slept like crap my first night in Salem would be the biggest understatement of all time.

It wasn't just the tiny bed. That would have been one thing. I could have dealt with that. No, it was mostly sleeping in the same bed with Mitch that made the night crappy. Some of the blame should go to Spencer, too, because I had no idea that anyone could snore that loud. It sounded like a chainsaw was running the entire night.

Thankfully Mitch doesn't snore, but he did try to get a little… frisky, during the night. I tried to be quiet, when telling him no, so that we didn't wake up Spencer. Mitch responded by grumbling, rolling over, and forcing me to the edge of the bed.

I waited until Mitch was asleep, took my pillow and put it on the floor and that's when I finally fell asleep. Noise coming from the hallway woke me up some time around six as the football players got ready for their morning practice.

I'm not going to just let what happened last night go. I'm going to have to talk to Mitch about it, especially since yesterday, again, we had a conversation about waiting to have sex. Maybe his eagerness has something to do with trying to be macho around the other football players.

It's too early and I'm too tired to have that conversation with Mitch this morning, so I pretend to be asleep as he gets ready and leaves. Spencer leaves just after Mitch and I wait for a few minutes, to make sure they aren't coming back and I climb into bed and pull the covers over my head.

I close my eyes and try to force myself to sleep. It's just not happening. There's a bright light shining through the window of the room, like some sort of reflection. After a few minutes of trying to sleep with my face in the pillow, as a last resort, I finally get up and go to the window to see what the heck is causing the reflection.

Even holding my hand up, to block the sun, it takes a minute for me figure out what it is. It's one of those sun visors, for car windshields, and the sun is hitting at just the perfect angle the reflection to blast its way into the room. The room without any kind of curtains. I guess they don't worry too much about football players wanting to sleep in or needing privacy.

As I stand there, wondering who could possibly be so inconsiderate as to blind me with their sunshade, I see a guy walking to the driver's door. I wait as he gets in and pulls the shade down.

I finally get a good look at him. It's Logan and he's looking right at me. Our eyes lock for a brief moment before I can duck to the floor.

"I wonder if he saw me?"

I don't know why I'm talking out loud or even asking myself that question. Of course he saw me.

I wait for a few minutes, just to be safe, realizing that he was probably on his way to practice and wasn't going to be waiting outside to see if he could catch another glimpse of me. The more I think about it, the dumber it sounds. I peek out the window, still trying to stay low and out of sight, and I don't see his SUV anymore. I stand up and brush myself off.

Even though I could use a shower, there's no way I'm going to risk that, not when I don't have anyone to watch the door for me. It's just not going to happen. I'm not ashamed of my body or anything, it's just that I don't particularly feel like giving a show to any of these young football players. Not to mention Mitch would probably freak out.

I head to the bathroom, with my toothbrush and quickly brush my teeth and wash my face. I risk it, since no one has come in yet and go pee. I hurry out of the bathroom and go back to the room to change.

I put on jeans and a T-shirt, newer ones, and head out. I need to find a job today, there's no way around it. I can't keep staying here with Mitch, and even though I have enough money to probably get me started with a place to live, I can't spend it until I have a job.

My best bet is heading down the same road where I went yesterday, to see if any of the places had help wanted signs up and if that failed I would just start going into places and asking for the manager. I don't like the idea of having to do that, but I don't have a choice right now.

Today, when I pass Burgers-R-Us, I notice that there is a help wanted sign in the window. I don't really want to work there, they seem slow and I don't want to get stuck being trained by the girl that waited on me yesterday, she reminds me too much of Rachel from the diner and that's almost enough to dissuade me from even going inside. Almost.

Yesterday when I kept walking, it seemed like none of the other restaurants were hiring, so Burgers-R-Us might really be my only choice. It doesn't matter, Amy, it's just a job. Suck it up and make some money. The sign on the door says they open at ten, so I check my phone and see that's it's two minutes after ten.

I put a smile on my face, open the door and walk inside. The restaurant, just like yesterday when I left, is empty. I guess it's kind of early and they did just open.

This is actually the best time to apply for a job. It also occurs to me, that unlike the diner, this place isn't open for breakfast, so if I did get a job here, I wouldn't have to wake up so ridiculously early like I did when I was working breakfast back in Greenville.

There's two employees, standing near the entrance to the kitchen. When they see me, the younger one goes into the kitchen and the older one walks over to me.

"Table for one?"

I shake my head and turn around and point to the sign in the window.

"I wanted to apply for the job."

"Great!"

He scurries off and comes back a minute later with a pen and an application.

"Sit wherever," he says.

I sit at the closest table and he stands a few feet away, I guess in case I have questions. The application is pretty straight forward, mostly just personal information and past work experience. I fill it out in five minutes and hand it back to him.

He quickly reads it over, nodding the entire time and then pulls out the chair across from me and sits down.

"Amy?"

"Yeah."

"So, you're from Greenville?"

"Yeah, I just moved here yesterday."

"Good, good."

He looks down at my application again.

"So how come you left your last job?"

I'm not even sure how to answer that. Obviously I can't tell him what really happened. The real story is so crazy that I'm not sure if anyone would even believe it.

"I… I moved for school."

"OK, good."

He looks up and down the application again and then sets it down on the table.

"Everything looks good. How soon can you start?"

I'm a little surprised given the fact that my only work experience is a month at the diner in Greenville.

"I can start whenever."

"Great," he says, standing up from the table and beckoning me to follow. "Let's get you set up and you can start by working the lunch shift today, if you want."

"Yeah, I can work today."

I stand up and follow him to the back of the restaurant. I glance into the kitchen as we walk past the open door and the guy I saw when I came in, who is actually the same guy who was working yesterday when I ate here, gives me a disgusted look and turns away. OK....

He leads me into the office and starts to look through the drawers of a faded, olive green file cabinet. The room is small, just wide enough to fit the old desk and chair and a file cabinet in each of the corners. The lack of window and natural light, makes it feel even smaller.

"Oh," he says, his head buried in a drawer, "I'm Gary, by the way."

"Nice to meet you, Gary."

"I'm the manager. I've been here for seven years and I started here just like you, walking in off the street and getting a job on my first day. Now look at me."

I cringe. I hope that I never get stuck in this kind of job for that long. Hopefully he doesn't read anything into my lack of a response... I'm just not even sure what to say to that, other than maybe 'I'm sorry.'

"Found it!"

His enthusiasm is remarkable. Gary spins around with a W-4 tax form. He hands it to me and waits as I grab a pen from his desk and fill it out, the same that I filled it out for the diner. I hand it back to him when I'm done and he puts it on top of a stack of papers in the middle of the desk.

Gary looks me up and down, turns around and

opens one of the drawers in the other file cabinet. He pulls out a half apron, the same style and color, black, that the girl yesterday was wearing.

"Here, put this on and follow me."

I step out of the office and follow him back into the dining room, tying on the apron as I go.

"What you're wearing is fine for today, but from now on, we need you to wear a black polo and black pants."

He leads me to the service area. Most of it looks familiar and I shouldn't have too much difficulty getting it all figured out.

"Are you going to be training me?"

"Oh, no. I actually need to duck out of here for a few hours, but you should be able to handle it on your own. If you have any questions, just use your best judgment or you can ask Dan, he's the cook that's working lunch today."

"Is it just the two of us working?"

I look around the dining room. There're enough tables and chairs to seat at least forty people. I can't handle that many tables by myself and I doubt that one cook could make food quickly enough, either.

"Yeah, but lunch is pretty slow. You probably won't get more than a couple of tables. It's not a big deal. Once the school year starts, then we will have more staff on for all the shifts, though."

"OK."

I'm not sure what else to do other than to agree. This is a little crazy, but I guess I'll just do what I can and hope that it doesn't get too busy.

"So, let me just show you how the cash register works," he says, glancing down at his watch. "Then I'm going to get out of here, but I'll be back by three and then you can go home."

I take a deep breath. You can do this, Amy, how hard can it be.

~~~~

My first shift at Burgers-R-Us was actually even less eventful than Gary had predicted. Not a single table came in while he was gone. He didn't get back until four, which was a little irritating, because by then I was bored out of my mind, cleaning everything in the dining room three times.

I guess I shouldn't really complain though, it's a job and so far it seems like it's going to be super easy and by the time it does actually get busy, there will be other servers. By then I should be able to learn the menu and become comfortable with how things work there.

I take my time walking back. I'm not exactly excited to be back in the cramped room. I'm really not looking forward to sleeping on the floor for a second night.

Maybe tomorrow, after work, I can start to look for an apartment.

Just a few minutes before I get back, a girl walks down the sidewalk of one of the houses on the street and pushes a sign into the grass next to the sidewalk and heads back inside. I stop in my tracks when I get close enough to read the sign. It says 'Room for Rent' and has a phone number. It's worth a shot.

I don't both calling the number, especially since she just put the sign out. I walk up to the door of the little yellow house and knock. I hear footsteps coming and I stand back. The door swings open, it's the girl that put the sign out, and she smiles at me.

"Can I help you?"

"Uh, yeah," I say, as I turn around and point at the sign. "I saw the sign and I wanted to ask about the room for rent."

A look of surprise crosses her face.

"Oh… wow… I wasn't expecting anyone that quickly. Come on in."

She stands to the side and I walk in. The house, from what I can see, is small but it's really nicely decorated and it's cute. I like it already.

"Here," she says. "Take a seat."

I follow her into the living room. I sit on the black leather couch and she sits across from me in a matching chair.

"What's your name?"

"Amy."

"I'm Jessica, but you can call me Jess."

"Nice to meet you."

"You too, Amy. So, are you a student?"

Every time someone asks me or mentions college I feel a twinge of pain. I still can't believe that I didn't get into State.

"I'm actually going to be going to the community college this year and transferring, next year. My boyfriend is going to State though and he's on the football team."

She perks up.

"Oh yeah? Does he have any cute friends?"

I laugh. I like her already. She seems nice and I instantly feel comfortable being around her.

"I don't know, I just got here yesterday, actually."

"Ah, gotcha. Well, down to business I guess. I've got an extra room, that I'm looking to rent for the year. It's four hundred, which includes all the utilities and cable and Internet and all that stuff."

It's a little more than I was hoping to pay for sharing a place with someone. Not to mention I've only ever lived with my parents and don't know what to expect really. She seems cool though and I think we would get along really well. If I keep making no tips at work, like today, it might be a little bit of a stretch, but I guess I could always try to find a second job if things don't pick up there soon.

"Can I see the room?"

She hops up from the chair.

"Of course! Come with me."

She leads me into the back of the house, where the two bedrooms are. There's one in each of the back corners of the house, with a bathroom separating them. We head into the room on the right. There's a bed against the far wall and a dresser, too.

"This place came furnished, so I hope you don't mind the style."

"It's totally fine."

The furniture is more than fine, it's much nicer than anything that we ever had at home. I'm starting to feel, for the first time in months, that things are starting to look up.

"So do you have a job?"

"Yeah," I say. "I just got a job at Burgers-R-Us. It's within walking distance."

"Nice, I know about it, but I've never been there. Do you have any single, male co-workers?"

We both laugh.

"There's only one guy that was working today, and I didn't really talk to him and I saw him kissing one of the other waitresses when I was there yesterday."

"Of course, just my luck."

We head back to the living room and sit down.

"I'm not like crazy or anything, I just got out of a relationship a couple of weeks ago and I'm like it's time to get back out there."

"Well, I'll let you know if I think of anyone."

"Thanks. So, anyway, when do you want to move in?"

Yay! I have a feeling that this is going to be great and I've just made a friend that I'm going to have for a long time.

"Is today too soon?"

"Not at all. Where are you staying right now?"

"I'm staying with my boyfriend, but he's just got a single bed and has a roommate, so I'm totally ready to get out of there."

"Uh, god, I hear ya. Do you have a car?"

"No, I just walk everywhere, or Mitch, my boyfriend, gives me rides."

"Do you want me to go help you get your stuff?"

"I think I'm good, I can get Mitch to help me with it once he gets back from practice. He's staying at the football housing place, which is just a few minutes away, and I don't have that much stuff, but I don't really want to carry it all that way."

"So… there's other football players staying there, too?"

"Yeah, I think most of the team is."

"So I know you don't need my help, but can I help you anyway?"

We both laugh, again. She's ridiculous. I have a feeling we might be getting ourselves into a little bit of trouble, every so often, and I kind of like the idea of that.

CHAPTER THIRTEEN

We get into Jessica's car, and it feels weird riding in so low to the ground after being in Mitch's truck and my brief ride in Logan's SUV. It's really comfortable and I almost wish that we weren't just driving right down the street.

There's a spot right in the front, that she easily backs into, I guess because she thinks that I must have a lot of stuff. I really could have just walked back and had Mitch give me a ride or walked, my stuff isn't that heavy, but Jess seemed so excited about going with me, so I couldn't say no.

I quickly look around the parking lot, to see if Mitch is back yet, and I spot his truck near the far end. I find myself, without really thinking about it, also looking for Logan's SUV, and when I don't see it I feel a little disappointed. I'm not sure why. I feel bad, still, about running out when we were eating dinner and since I'm leaving, and probably won't be seeing him again, ever, I feel like I need to apologize and explain myself.

We head inside, Jess right behind me, and I knock on Mitch's door. I look up and down the hall as we wait, sure that at any moment Logan is going to show up. Mitch opens the door to the room and we go in. His eyes widen at the sight of Jess.

"Who's this?"

"Oh," I say, "Jess, this is Mitch, my boyfriend, Mitch this is Jess."

"Nice to meet you," he says.

She nods and smiles as she looks around the room.

"So, what's up? Where have you been today?"

Whoops. I guess I forgot to text him and tell him about Burgers-R-Us. The thought had crossed my mind, a few times actually, but I was so wrapped up in my day of work.

"Yeah… sorry. I got a job today, not too far away."

"Oh, good," he says. "So I guess that means you can move out soon."

His voice has a weird tone to it. I can't quite figure out if he's irritated, or something else entirely. Weird. I almost get the feeling that he was maybe expecting me to stay here longer. I'm not really sure what to think about it, so I quickly push the thoughts out of my mind.

"Yeah… actually, that's what Jess is doing here. I wasn't sure if you had time to help me, so she offered to drive my stuff back to her place."

Mitch raises his eyebrows and looks at Jess. I can tell now, for sure, that he's not happy about the whole situation. It doesn't make sense though. I just assumed that when he helped me get out of Greenville, that he wanted me to get a job and a place to live. Why is he acting so strange right now?

Without saying anything, Mitch pulls my duffel bags out from under his bed, hands one of them to each of us and then gives me my small bag of other stuff. Jess and I look at each other. I'm glad I'm not the only one who thinks his behavior is weird.

"Well, I've got a football meeting soon, so I guess you should probably go."

"OK… well, I'll text you later."

He opens the door and waits for us to leave.

"Sure, whatever."

Once we get outside, I start to laugh. Not because it's funny, but I have no idea what's wrong with Mitch and I don't know how else to respond.

"Alright, well, he seems sad to see me go."

"Yeah… that was kind of weird."

We both start to laugh. I know he will get over it, whatever it is, and then we will talk about it and things will go back to normal. That's how it always goes when he's in a mood, like this. He probably had a bad day at practice or something.

"What's so funny?"

I recognize the voice this time. Logan. Amy and I both turn. He's walking toward us, coming from his SUV. He clicks the button on his remote and the lights on the car flash behind him as he walks toward us. I feel like I'm watching a slow motion scene from a movie, where the good looking guy walks to the girl.

Without thinking, I do exactly what my mind told me not to do and I smile at Logan. He flashes his pearly white grin back.

"Amy, who's your friend?"

"Uh… this… this…."

"Jessica, but my friends call me Jess."

"Nice to meet you, I'm Logan."

Jess elbows me and I know what she's thinking.

"So," he says, turning to me. "What happened at dinner? You just kind of disappeared…."

She elbows me again.

"Uh… yeah, sorry about that, I got an urgent phone call when I was in the bathroom."

I cringe at the lie and hope that he doesn't notice. Even though I still feel really bad about running out on him like that, there's no way I will ever tell him why I left.

"I see. Well, you look like you're busy, I won't

keep you."

"Maybe we will see you around?" Jess says.

With his eyes still on me, he nods his head.

"You ladies should come to a game this year, they're a lot of fun."

"We will."

Jess nudges me.

"Yeah, we'll be there." I say.

"Well, I'll see you soon."

Logan winks at me, turns and walks inside. We start walking to Jess's car and she starts to giggle uncontrollably.

"What?"

"He so wants you."

My face turns bright red. I doubt that. He's just trying to be nice, like when he took me out to eat. I'm surprised he even wanted to talk to me after what I did. I have a feeling the only reason he came over to us is because he saw Jess.

"No, I think he was just being friendly."

"Yeah, he wants to be *really friendly* with you."

I blush again as we get into the car. I look over at Jess and she starts to laugh. She starts the car and we head back to the house.

"Sorry," she says. "I'm just teasing you, but he definitely likes you."

"That's part of the problem. We went out to dinner, which I thought was just a friendly meal. As it went on, I started to get the feeling that it was something different. He asked if I had a boyfriend and I panicked and ran out of the back of the restaurant."

"Seriously?"

"Yeah, I know, right. I'm so lame."

"You should have just told him, it's not that big of a deal."

"Maybe you're right."

"I'm really just trying to distract you and remind

you that you have a boyfriend so that I can pounce on Logan."

She's ridiculous. I force myself not to laugh. Did she really just say she wants to pounce on him?

"How come you didn't mention Logan when I asked if you knew any guys that you could hook me up with?"

Now that I think of it, I'm not really sure why I didn't think to mention Logan.

"I don't know, I guess I forgot about him."

"You forgot about him?"

"Yeah. Why?"

"I'll never forget him," she says.

We both laugh as she parks the car in front of the house and we get out. She grabs one of the duffel bags, I get the rest, and we head inside. We take my bags to my bedroom and set them on the floor. I'll unpack later.

"So, what's the deal with Logan? Dish."

We head into the living room and sit on the couch.

"What do you mean?"

"I want to know everything you know about him."

"Well, there isn't much really... I've only talked to him twice, including today."

"Really?"

"I guess it's more like two and a half times."

"How did you talk to him a half of a time?"

I shouldn't have said that. I don't want to tell her what I meant. It's too late though and I think she's not going to stop asking until I tell her.

"When I first got to the football housing, I really had to pee and there's no women's bathrooms."

"Oh, my, god. Did you see *it*?"

"What?"

"You know, his...."

My face gets hot and I shake my head.

"That's unfortunate," she says.

113

Not exactly what I was thinking.

"What happened was I didn't realize there was no Women's room and Mitch told me the bathroom was down the hall, so I just walked into the bathroom without looking at the sign on the door and Logan was standing there, with just a towel wrapped around his… his bottom half."

My face still feels warm.

"That's hot. I bet he looks fab without his shirt on."

I shrug.

"Oh, come on," she says.

He did look good and there was no way I was ever going to admit that to her. I was having a hard enough time admitting to myself. I felt bad, almost like I was being unfaithful to Mitch just for thinking it.

"And then what happened?"

"That was kind of it. I closed my eyes and left and then he saw me in the hallway and I ran back to Mitch's room."

"Wait, so are you telling me that you ran away from him in the bathroom, in the hallway and then a third time at a restaurant."

It sounds so much worse when she says it.

"Yeah…"

"So you ran away from him every time you saw him, other than today."

"Yeah."

"Jesus, you're such a spazz."

I shrug. I can't explain it, especially with how comfortable and calm being around him made me feel. I wasn't about to mention that to Jess though. I know that I would never hear the end of it. I still might not.

"It's a good thing you have a boyfriend or I would smack you."

We laugh. I hope that I wouldn't act this way around Logan if I was single, but I don't know for sure.

"What does Mitch think about you and Logan?"

"What do you mean?"

I shift my weight on the couch, trying to find a more comfortable spot. I have a feeling we aren't going anywhere anytime soon.

"I mean, does Mitch know about you and Logan. Like, did you tell him that you went out to dinner with Logan?"

I shake my head. It does sound kind of bad. I wish now that I had thought about it before. I hope that Mitch doesn't find out. I know he would be pissed.

"Are they friends?"

"I don't know, I haven't been here long enough to know."

"But they're both on the football team, right?"

"Yeah, they are."

"Hmm, well… it could be awkward if Mitch finds out."

That's putting it gently. I wasn't that worried about it before, but now that Jess has mentioned it, I'm starting to worry a little bit. Hopefully now that I'm living here, I won't run into Logan anymore and Mitch won't find out.

"Yeah," I say. "It could be, really, not good."

"You can't worry about it now."

She's right. There's no point. It will just stress me out, wondering if Mitch knows about what happened between Logan and me. Nothing really happened, obviously, but that might not stop Mitch from being suspicious and mad and I definitely don't want that, not after everything he's done for me recently.

I let out a sigh and force a smile at Jess.

"Don't worry," she says. "I'm sure it's fine. What's the worst that could happen?"

The most famous last words of all time.

~~~~

I sit down in my room after I finish unpacking and look around. It's not quite homey yet, but it'll get there. It's a heck of a lot better than sharing a tiny bed with Mitch and having to listen to Spencer snoring all night.

Jess loaned me some sheets and a pillow until I get my own. I realize now how much I really didn't think ahead. I didn't bring anything other than clothes and some basic toiletries. Not exactly planning ahead.

Now that I really have some privacy for the first time since leaving Greenville, I figure this is as good a time as any to check the three voicemails from my dad. That little number three on the screen on my phone has been taunting me and I can't take it anymore.

I punch up the first voicemail, which came just after the second text.

"Amy, you didn't text me back, so I'm leaving you this message instead. Listen, we need to talk, it's important. I know that you're mad at me… And I get it, I really do. I was an idiot and an ass and I want to make it up to you. Just call me back, sweetheart. Everything will work out, it always does."

I'm actually a little surprised by the tone of his call. I was expecting him to be a little more upset based on what happened and the note that I left for him. I have a feeling, though, that just like his texts, the tone of the messages is going to change. I put my phone up to my ear as the second one starts to play.

"It's Dad, again. I know that you have your phone, you never go anywhere without it. You need to call me, this is a little ridiculous. Look, Amy, I know you're upset at me and your mother, but don't act like this all my fault, OK? Please, just call me back, we really need to sit down and have a conversation."

I cringe. That was more along the lines that I was expecting. I'm not looking forward to listening to the last one. He's right, I'm upset at Mom and at him and it isn't all his fault, it's hers too and it's also the fault of State. If I had just gotten in, everything might have been different, but I know there's no point in wondering 'what if.' I punch up the last voicemail.

"Alright, this is ridiculous. I'm your father. I raised you. I put a roof over your head. I did everything for you. You don't get to just run off with Mitch and play house. That's not how the world works. You need to get your shit together, Amy, and get your ass back here or we are going to have a serious problem. Call me back, right now. There are going to be some serious consequences if you don't."

I drop my phone onto the bed as tears flow down my cheeks. I've never heard so much anger in his voice and it scares me, not to mention that by the last message he was slurring his words so bad that it was amazing he could actually be standing still. If he was trying to get me to come home… well, after listening to those voicemails, I really don't care if I ever see him again.

There's no way I'm calling him back. After what he's put me through, I don't care that he's my dad, he doesn't deserve to have me in his life and I don't need him anymore. I curl up on the bed and wipe the tears from my eyes. I hope that Jess doesn't hear me crying. The last thing that I need is my newest friend thinking that I'm a total drama queen and emotional wreck.

When I finally calm down, I pick my phone up. I need to talk to Mitch. After going through the voicemails from my dad, I need to talk to someone who cares and who gets me and even though today was a little weird with Mitch, I know that he will get it.

Hey, how are you? I miss you.

I wait for a reply. There isn't one after a few minutes, so I text him again. Maybe he didn't hear his phone.

I want to talk to you, if you're free. I just listened to some voicemails that my dad left me.

Again there's no reply. Maybe he's in a football meeting or his phone is off. I wait for a few minutes, which seem to drag on forever and I text him again.

Just text me or call me when you get this. Xoxo.

I set my phone down, expecting to not get a reply anytime soon, but my phone chips almost instantly. I pick it up and read the text from Mitch.

I don't have anything to say to you.

Baffled by what I just read, I read it again to make sure my eyes aren't playing tricks on me.

What? Did you mean to send that to me?

He must have meant to send it to someone else. Mitch would never send me something like that, not on purpose. I wonder who he could be talking to though.

Yes, Amy, I meant to send that to you. I don't want to talk to you.

Why is he doing this? I don't get it. I didn't do or say anything that should have upset him this much. He was in a weird mood today, when I brought Jess over. Could he really be this mad because I found a job and a place to live?

Are you mad because I moved today?

I tap my foot on the wood floor as I wait for a response.

No, it has nothing to do with that. Stop texting me, I'm done.

Done? What is he talking about? Done with what? Tears start to fill my eyes. Mitch is my rock, he's the only one that gets me and he's been there for me through this whole year. He was so supportive when Mom left and rushed to Greenville to rescue me. What changed in one day?

Mitch, don't do this. You're scaring me.

Tears start to fall from my eyes. Rushing down my cheek, they drop and splash on the floor as I cry.

I saw you, with him. Spencer told me that someone saw you two eating dinner the other night. I didn't believe him at first, I told

him he was full of shit. We got into a huge fight. And then today…
I saw you talking to him and I knew.

No. This can't be happening. I knew that I never should have gone to dinner with Logan. I was just so upset about my dad and he had just been there at the right moment in time to lend me some kindness, when Mitch wasn't around. That wasn't his fault though, he was at practice. I can't believe how stupid I was.

Please, let me come over and explain. It isn't what you think it is. There's nothing going on with Logan, I swear to you.

My fingers are shaking so badly that I barely manage to hit send.

No. Don't you dare come over. We are done. Now don't text me, ever again.

My phone falls from my hand and slides across the floor. I smash my face into my pillow and scream as I punch the bed as hard as I can.

This can't be happening.

CHAPTER FOURTEEN

I don't know if it's possible for my life to suck any more than it does today.

I barely slept last night. When I did, my dreams were filled with Mitch and my dad, the two men in my life. I can't talk to my dad, he is so out of control that I don't know that I'll ever have a relationship with him again and Mitch, who is pissed at me for something I didn't really do.

Even though nothing happened with Logan, after my conversation with Mitch, I feel guilty and I feel worse with each passing hour. I have this feeling, in the deepest part of my soul, that Mitch will never forget this or forgive me. I can't imagine my life without him. I don't care what he said last night, I'm going over there today and I'm going to explain to him what really happened and he is going to take me back. He has to.

I was up early, not wanting to sleep anymore, watching the clock and waiting for it to be late enough for Mitch to be awake. I heard Jess moving around in the kitchen and I decided to wait a little longer. I didn't want to run into her this morning. I'm sure she heard me crying last night and if she didn't she must have heard me scream. I don't think I can tell her what happened. I need to speak to Mitch first.

I check my phone, but there're no messages from Mitch. Thankfully after that first group of texts and voicemails, my dad has stopped, too. I don't think I could deal with that right now.

It's late enough in the morning that Mitch is probably at practice now, so I'm just going to have to wait until after work to talk to him. I hop in the shower and let the warm water cascade over my head. It's nice to take a shower and not have to worry about some guy walking into the bathroom.

I get out of the shower, dry myself off and get dressed for work. This time wearing the black pants and shirt that Gary said was the standard uniform for the employees of Burgers-R-Us. I don't have to be at work for forty-five minutes, which should give me enough time to eat. I really need to get to the grocery store, to get some basic stuff, but until then Jess said I could have whatever I want out of the fridge.

I feel kind of bad about eating her food, but she insisted that she didn't mind at all. I open the fridge and look through it. There's a decent amount of food, definitely more than was in my fridge at home once Mom left, but nothing is really sounding that good. I have no appetite really. The whole thing with Mitch has left me feeling so crappy. I pull out a plain bagel, take a bit out of it and grab my purse and head out of the house. At least it will give me something in my stomach while I work. If I get hungry later I can always eat there.

Gary is standing by the front door when I get to Burger-R-Us, at a quarter to ten, and he holds the door open and follows me inside.

"How are you?" he says.

"I'm good, how are you?"

I'm awful actually. I seriously doubt that Gary wants to hear about all of my life problems, now or ever, so I do my best to smile and attempt to hide my emotions.

"Oh, well, my mom's in the hospital again, so I was just coming in to open and then leave. It shouldn't be busy today, so I'll come back at two or so and then you can go home."

So much for keeping personal problems to yourself. I can't believe for the second day in a row there will be no one else working who can train me and teach me about the menu.

"Is she OK?"

He shrugs and tries to smile, but there is a definite sadness behind it.

"She'll be fine."

His voice quakes as he says it. I have a feeling that even though he's saying it, he doesn't really believe it. It's sad. I hope, even though I know nothing about her, that she will be OK and that she can make a full recovery.

"Anyway," he says, "I hope you don't mind me leaving."

"Of course not."

"I'll be back by two, I promise."

He leaves, turning on the open sign as he does. I doubt he'll be on time, seeing as how he was late yesterday. I can't blame him though, this is an actual emergency. I wonder why he doesn't just take time off of work and have someone cover for him.

"Hey."

I turn around and Dan is standing by the door to the kitchen, leaning against the wall.

"Yeah?"

"I was just saying hello."

"Oh… hey."

"Where did Gary go?"

"His mom is in the hospital. He said he would be back by two."

Dan pulls out his phone, taps a few keys and slides it back into his pocket.

"Well, this is exciting," he says.

I nod in agreement. I really hope that it starts to get busier soon, or that maybe I can work a few night shifts, too. I really need the money right now, especially if I'm going to pay for classes at the community college this fall.

Dan turns and goes back into the kitchen. I miss working with Dylan, at the diner. He was at least nice and would hang out and talk about whatever when it was slow. I guess to be fair I don't know Dan, maybe he's just shy or something.

The door chime goes off and I spin around, excited to finally have my first customer. It's a young woman, maybe a couple of years older than me and she looks familiar, but I can't quite place it.

"I'm here for my final check."

That's who she is. She's the girl who waited on me the day before I got the job, the one who was awful and making out with Dan in the kitchen.

"Gary's not here right now. He should be back by two, though."

She lets out an irritated sigh.

"Dan!"

He pops out of the kitchen and walks over to us.

"Hey, what's up?"

"The new girl won't give me my check and she said Gary is gone."

"Gimme one sec."

Dan goes into the office and comes out a minute later with a white envelope and hands it to her.

"Thanks, I'll see you tonight."

He leans in and they share a quick kiss. Dan steps back and she gives me a dirty look before turning and strutting out of the restaurant. Huh. That was weird. I turn to ask Dan about it, but he's already back in the kitchen. Whatever, I don't have time to worry about why she seemed irritated by my mere presence.

I take the next twenty minutes to wipe down the

tables and the chair legs in the dining room, when the door chime goes off. I smile at the four girls as I walk over to them, with menus in my hand.

"Four of you?"

"Yes, four." says the blond one.

"This way."

"She can count," one of them says, doing her best to whisper. I still hear her.

I lead them to a table that I pick at random and wait for them to sit down, but they sit at the next table over. They start to giggle as if what they had just done was so funny. I brush it off and set their menus down on the table and go to get them water.

I take a deep breath. It's just another table, your first table at this job, so do a good job and try to be nice no matter what. Normally I don't worry about customers, but I could already tell that these girls were going to be a handful. I pull out my order pad and walk over to them.

"Are you ladies ready to order?"

None of them say anything and instead look at the blond one.

"We want an order of onion rings, an order of fries and a house salad with extra blue cheese dressing."

"Anything else?"

The blond girl just stares at me. The look on her face suggests that I'm in some way inconveniencing her. I turn and walk to the kitchen. I tear the order off my pad and hand it to Dan. He reads it over and then hangs it on an order strip above the prep area.

"Gimme five minutes and I'll have your order ready."

I head back into the dining room. The girls have moved tables and start to giggle when they notice me looking at them. I head over to the service station and pull out my phone while I wait for the food. No messages. I really want to text Mitch, he's probably back from his morning practice by now. I resist the temptation and instead flip through the pictures of us on my phone.

I get halfway through the pictures when I hear the bell ding to announce that my food is ready. I take one last look at the picture of Mitch and me at the lake during spring break. We looked so happy.

I carry the three plates to the table of girls, who has moved again and is now at their third table and set them down in the middle, assuming that they are sharing.

"Can I get you anything else?"

"Um... yeah, we need some plates to share with."

The tone of her voice is so irritated that I almost want to not give them any plates. They are just tormenting me on purpose. I take a deep breath and go get the plates. Calm down, Amy, they are customers and customers are always right. I set a plate down in front of each girl and smile at them.

"Are you all set?"

"We didn't order *this*," the blonde says, pointing at the salad.

"I'm sorry?"

"This salad. I said dressing on the side."

The customer is always right. The customer is always right. I feel like if I say it over and over then I won't scream.

"Of course you did. That was my mistake. Let me take this one back and I'll get you a new salad."

"Thanks."

It's a hollow thank you. I know she knows that she ordered a salad with extra dressing and not on the side. I understand that sometimes people make mistakes and don't order the right thing, but I know exactly what she said.

I set the salad down in the kitchen. Dan turns to me and frowns.

"What's wrong with it?"

"She says that she wanted a salad with dressing on the side, not extra dressing."

He lets out a groan and pulls another plate from the shelf and starts to re-make it.

"Sorry."

"No worries," he says. "These girls come in here all the time and they always give us a hard time."

"Why doesn't Gary do something about it?"

Dan just laughs.

"The blond one, the one who I'm assuming is the one giving you a hard time, is the daughter of the owners. She can do whatever she wants."

Great. Now I know that not only do I have to be extra nice to her, but I'm not going to even get a tip for putting up with them.

"Ugh."

"Exactly," Dan says.

He finishes the salad, puts the dressing in a container on the side and hands it to me.

"Thanks."

"No problem. Don't let them get to you. She's going to do her best to get you to quit or do something stupid enough that they will have to fire you. Don't let her win."

"Thanks."

I head out of the kitchen and back to their table, and put a huge smile on my face as I set the salad down.

"I'm ever so sorry about that, I can't believe I did that. Please let me know if there's anything else I can get you."

She waves me off with her fork. Someone needs to teach this girl some manners. I go back to the service area and pull out my phone again. I need to think about what I'm going to say to Mitch. He has to take me back, there's no way that after all we've been through that he would really break up with me over a misunderstanding.

"Waitress!"

Ugh. Now what. I put my phone in my pocket and go back to the table of needy girls. There's a huge puddle of water in the middle of their table and they are all just sitting there, staring at it and not even trying to soak it up with their napkins. I rush back to the service station and grab two rags and clean up the mess. They don't even apologize or thank me for it. I force myself to take a deep breath and to smile at them as much as I can. There's no way I'm going to let her cost me my job. I don't care what she does, she's not going to break me.

The girls finally leave after a few more minutes, not even bothering to say anything or pay for their food. I guess that since her parents own it she doesn't have to pay, but since I'm new and Gary isn't here, it would have been nice for her to say something. I bus their table and find two pennies on the table.

I would love to give them my two cents.

I head into the kitchen with the plates and put them in the sink.

"Who does the dishes?"

"Someone will come in later to do the dishes from the whole day, so just put them in the sink."

I head back into the dining room and clean and reset the three tables the girls managed to mess up. I'm just glad they're gone. I really hope that they don't make a habit of coming in when I'm working.

The rest of my shift is boring really, consisting of just wiping down the menus and trying to find odd cleaning jobs. I refill the salt and pepper shakers and then the ketchup on all the tables. By the time I finish, it's two, but there's no sign of Gary. I head into the kitchen to see what Dan is doing, just so that I have something to do. He's chopping carrots and tossing them in a soup pot that's on the stove.

"What are you making?"

"Soup."

"What kind?"

"Chicken noodle."

I stand there, watching him. He's not much of a

conversationalist. I'm actually a little envious of the fact that he always seems to have some sort of work to do. Not that I would want to work in the kitchen, but I'm feeling bored right now.

"Do you need something?"

"No... I just ran out of things to clean and Gary isn't back yet."

Dan laughs.

"Of course he isn't, he's always late. Two means three."

"Great..."

"You got places to be or something?"

I do actually, but I'm not about to tell Dan my life story.

"I just want to go home, it's been a long day."

"Do you want something to eat?"

The door chime goes off.

"I'm fine, thanks."

I head into the dining room and see Gary walking toward me. I guess it's a good sign that he's here, he wouldn't come back to work if something truly awful had happened. I don't think.

"You can head out."

"Thanks."

I grab my purse and leave work. I'm curious to know if his mom is OK, but I didn't want to bring it up, and given our conversation this morning, I figure that if he wants to talk about it he will.

CHAPTER FIFTEEN

Jess is home when I get back from work, but her bedroom door is closed. I head into my room and change into shorts and a T-shirt. I check my phone again, for what seems like the hundredth time today and there's no texts from Mitch. I don't know why I keep checking. I guess maybe a part of me hopes that he will realize that he overreacted and he will ask me to explain what really happened.

I leave the house and start walking. I try to figure out what I'm going to say to Mitch, but I keep thinking about how last night he didn't even want me to explain it to him. He has to listen to me. I can't lose him, not now and not like this.

When I get there, Mitch's truck is in the parking lot. I also spot Logan's SUV. I head inside and look down both hallways, not wanting to run into Logan, but the coast is clear. I knock on Mitch's door and I hear shuffling inside the room, but no one answers the door.

I knock again and move my ear close to the door. I think I hear someone inside the room, whispering, but I can't tell who it is or what they are saying. I pull out my phone and call Mitch's number. I hear ringing from inside the room. So he's in there and he's not answering the door. He must know, somehow, that it's me. He silences his phone after the second ring and my call is sent to voicemail.

I take a step back from the door, unsure of what to do and I notice a sock on the doorknob. I have no idea why it's there, but it strikes me as quite odd. I reach for the sock.

"I wouldn't do that if I were you."

Logan. I pull my hand back and turn to face him. He's standing a few feet down the hall, just leaning against the wall, casually. I turn back to the door and reach for the sock again.

"Seriously, don't take the sock off."

I frown and turn back to him.

"Why not?"

Logan starts to laugh.

"You don't know what the sock is for, do you?"

I feel my face turning red in embarrassment. He's right, I have no idea why it's there. Should I?

"Just trust me. Come back later, alright?"

For some reason I believe him and I step away from the door. I walk toward him, he's between me and the door, and he steps into the middle of the hall as I approach.

"I was wondering if you want to have dinner sometime?"

I move around him and keep walking. I can't do this right now.

"Amy," Logan says.

I don't stick around to hear what he was going to say. I head outside and walk down the outside of the building. Mitch may not be answering my phone calls or opening his door, but I can still look through his window and try to get his attention. I really need to talk to him. I'm not giving up this easily.

"Amy!"

I hear footsteps behind me. I don't turn around, but in the matter of a few seconds Logan is walking next to me.

"Why are you playing hard to get?"

I stop and glare at him. He has a goofy smile on his face.

"I have a boyfriend. Why else would I be hanging out *here*."

His smile fades and is replaced by a sad look.

"I don't know. I thought maybe you had a brother who's on the team or something."

"No, my boyfriend is."

"That's why you ran out when we were having dinner the other night."

I nod and turn. He puts his hand on my arm before I start to walk.

"I still want to be friends with you," he says.

I twist my arm and pull away from him. I can't believe that with everything going on with Mitch right now, Logan suddenly wants to be my friend. How can he not get that I'm trying to talk to Mitch?

"Was that his room you were trying to get in to?"

I don't answer. I look across the parking lot, trying to figure out a landmark so that I know which window is Mitch's.

"Amy, stop. Don't look through that window."

I stop in front of the window and turn to Logan. His eyes are pleading with me. I don't understand why he's trying to stop me.

My phone starts to ring. I pull it out and my heart skips a beat when I see the screen. Mitch is calling me. I answer his call and put the phone up to my ear.

"Hey," I say.

I turn to Logan, but he's gone.

"What do you want?"

"I need to talk to you."

He doesn't answer, but he's still on the line.

"No."

"What do you mean, no?"

"I mean no. I have nothing else to say to you, Amy. I think that it's best that we both go our separate ways. It's time."

Tears roll down my cheek. Is this really happening?

"Please, Mitch, don't do this."

"Me? Don't make me the bad guy. You did this."

"Nothing happened, I swear Mitch. Just let me explain it to you, I swear, nothing happened with Logan."

Mitch doesn't say anything.

"I would never cheat on you," I say, trying to talk through the tears. "It's just a misunderstanding. Please, Mitch."

"I saw how you looked at him. I've never even seen you look at me like that."

"What are you talking about?"

"Amy, I saw it, OK. You looked so happy and content when you were talking to him. I could see on your face that you're in love with him."

"What?"

"So I'm going to end this now, before you have a chance to hurt me anymore."

The line goes dead as Mitch hands up. I lean against the wall and slide down it until I'm sitting on the ground. I cover my face with my hands as I cry. I can't even think.

This can't really be happening. Mitch is the only bright spot in my life. He's my rock, he's my love, he's my future. He doesn't believe me though. I have to figure out a way to show him that I love only him.

I sit there, against the wall, crying, for I have no idea how long. Eventually the tears stop. I know there's nothing I can do. I just have to keep trying to show Mitch that I love him and that he's the only one for me.

I get up as the sun starts to set and slowly make

my way back to the house. I see Jess's car out front. I hope that she's in her room. I can't pretend to be in a good space, emotionally, right now and I don't think she would understand.

I walk through the door and Jess is sitting on the couch, reading a magazine. She looks at me and instantly shuts the magazine and sets it on the coffee table.

"Are you alright? Did something happen?"

"I'm… alright."

As soon as I finish talking I burst into tears.

"Come here, sit with me."

I shake my head and start toward my room.

"Amy, please? Just sit down, you don't have to tell me what's wrong, but you can't just shut yourself in your room. That won't solve anything."

I go back into the living room and sit down on the other end of the couch. Jess hands me a tissue. I dry my tears and blow my nose. We sit there for a few minutes, neither of us moving or saying anything. I want to tell her what happened, but I don't know… I just met her.

"You don't have to tell me what happened, but if you need to talk, I'm here for you. You can tell me anything."

She touches my arm and I do my best to smile as I force myself to not cry anymore.

"If this is about a man, screw him, tell me what happened, we'll eat pints of ice cream and forget this night. Tomorrow will be a new day."

She's right. Things will be better tomorrow. They have to be since they can't get any worse than this. I'm so glad that I met Jess, she's amazing.

I fill Jess in on everything that has happened in the last couple of days, only since I've moved here, while we sit on the couch. She just listens and nods every so often.

"That's pretty much it," I say.

"Well, I'm sorry, but Mitch sounds like the biggest

idiot in the world."

We both laugh. It feels good and I'm glad I told her what's going on. I feel a little better. I'm still really upset about Mitch, but if he's not going to talk to me or see me, there's not much I can do about it right now. I just need to give him some time.

"What do you think I should do?"

"About what?"

"Mitch. What can I do to get him to understand there's nothing going on with Logan? I feel like no matter how I told him, he didn't want to hear it."

"I don't know, Amy. Does it really matter?"

"What do you mean?"

"It sounds to me like he's already made up his mind. Mitch wants nothing to do with your explanation. And I'm assuming you figured out the sock on the door handle by now, right?"

"No, do you know what it is?"

She opens her mouth and closes it. I can tell that she knows and is hesitant about telling me.

"Please? Just tell me, Jess."

"Alright, but Logan was right. It's a good thing you didn't look through the window of Mitch's room."

"Wait, what?"

"The sock on the door knob, it means that someone in the room was getting *intimate*."

"Oh, god. I'm glad I didn't see that. I never need to see Spencer doing *that*."

Jess stares at me, the look on her face suggesting that I'm crazy.

"What? Why are you looking at me like that?"

"Amy, seriously? Think about it. You called his phone and you heard it ring in the room and there was a sock on the door. How much more obvious could it be?"

No. No. It can't be. There's no way it's possible. I feel like I'm going to cry, but I hold it in. I can't just keep crying in front of Jess. She leans over and wraps her arms around me and gives me a hug. When she lets go and sits back, her face says that she's sorry that she had to be the one to tell me.

"I don't… I don't get it. How could he accuse me of being unfaithful and the next day he's sleeping with some girl, already."

"Well, do you really want to know what I think?"

I nod. I'm in shock. I don't believe that Mitch would do this to me. There has to be some sort of explanation.

"I think that either he was getting back at you for something that he thought you did or he was already seeing her before and he had to break up with you so that she didn't find out about you."

"I don't know, Mitch is a good guy, he's not capable of doing something like that. We had a life plan, we were going to be together forever."

"It looks to me like he didn't want the same things as you."

I look down. I don't believe it. Could Mitch be capable of something like that? Not my Mitch, there was no way.

"I dunno, Jess, it's not like him."

"I'm just saying. If you look at the chain of events and the evidence, that's what it looks like to me. It's up to you to decide if you think that's what happened."

My heart tells me that Mitch would never hurt me like that and even though I just met Jess, I knew that she was probably right and I just couldn't face that. Not right now. Not after everything that has happened. I can't do it.

"I hate to be the one to say it," Jess says, "But maybe this is happening for a reason. My dad always says 'Jessica, everything happens for a reason. The universe has a plan for all of us, so just hang on, life is a wild ride.'"

"What reason could there possibly be for Mitch *dumping* me?"

Jess shrugs and looks at me. She doesn't have to

say it. I have a pretty good idea of what she's thinking and I don't like it. Not one bit.

CHAPTER SIXTEEN

I roll on my side and press the snooze button, for the third time. No one should ever get up this early.

"Come on, Amy, time to get up."

It's Jess, on the other side of my door, trying to get me up.

"In a minute."

I pull the covers back over my head. I made the mistake of sleeping with my door unlocked the first time I agreed to go for a morning run with Jess. That will never happen again. She came in my room and proceeded to shake me until I got up. It wasn't pretty.

"Amy, don't make me climb through one of your windows."

That did it. I left my windows open when I slept and I knew that she would follow through on her threat if I didn't get up and the last thing I needed was her climbing through my window at six in the morning.

I still don't know how she talked me into going running in the morning. She said that I couldn't stay in my room all day, to which I responded that I could and was planning on doing it.

I get up, stretch my arms and try to force myself

awake. I quickly put on my running shoes, shorts, sports bra and shirt. When I open my bedroom door, Jess was standing there, with a huge grin on her face.

"You look way too happy for this time of day."

"What? It's a beautiful morning and we are about to go for a run."

"Exactly."

I follow her outside and we stretch on the front lawn. I need to get loose if I want to have any chance of keeping up with her.

"Eventually you'll wonder how you ever made it this far in life without a morning run, I promise."

I start to laugh. I really doubt that.

"I'm serious," she says. "They have changed my life."

"Yeah?"

"A guy broke up with me junior year of high school and I was so depressed that I just stayed in my room for a week and didn't want to even eat. Well, I mean food. I ate plenty of ice cream."

"Yeah, and what part of that story is supposed to make me want to run? I would love to be in bed still, plotting my ice cream consumption for the day."

"I ate so much ice cream one day that I made myself sick. The next morning I woke up early and made myself go for a run. I have no idea why, it just seemed like I should do it and I've been running every morning since."

I let out a groan as I finish my stretches. I really doubt that this is going to be an everyday thing for me. Right now I feel obligated to at least humor Jess, given her kindness and willingness to let me rent a room from her.

"You ready?"

"As ready as I'm ever going to be."

She cracks a smile and takes off running. We head down a street that I've never been down, which just like all of our other morning runs, takes us nowhere near the football housing. I have a feeling that it's an intentional choice on her part.

I don't know what I would do if I saw Mitch right now. It's been a week, which I almost can't believe, and I feel like I'm finally starting to feel a little bit like my old self again. I think most of that, though, is because of Jess. She has just been amazing and so kind since I moved in.

"So, how's work?"

"It's work," I say. "You?"

I've already learned my lesson about making my words count during runs. The first day I talked too much and we had to stop every ten minutes for me to catch my breath. I'm not really in bad shape, I don't think, but can anything really prepare you for a three mile run when all you want to do is curl up in bed and cry?

"Eh, you know how it is."

Jess works at a bar and she insists that I need to get a job at one once I turn eighteen. The idea never really crossed my mind, but based on the kind of money she's making, it's definitely something I'll think about. What I don't understand is how she can work so late at night and still manage to get up this early to run, she's crazy.

"Yeah, good tips?" I say.

"I made two hundred last night."

Holy crap. I've barely made that in my whole first week at Burgers-R-Us.

"Wow. That's good."

She nods. We both are silent for the next half mile or so, trying to not talk too much. The world around us is still coming to life, which is one of the few things that I actually enjoy about our morning runs. There's something almost magical about it. The birds are chirping, squirrels are running across people's yards and climbing trees and there's beautiful flowers everywhere.

I sneeze. There's that too. Every time I get excited about trees and plants flowering, I start to sneeze. I sneeze again.

"You alright?" Jess says.

I wave her off as we keep running. I wonder though, because my allergies are so much worse here than they ever were in Greenville, if maybe it has something to do with the air quality here. I mean, it's not a big city, mostly just a college town, but there's still a lot more cars and pollution than in Greenville.

I slow down a little as I sneeze a third time. Jess slows down too.

"C'mon, the faster you run now, the sooner we will be done."

She's right, I just don't really want to think about it.

Jess turns down the street on our right and I follow, running just behind her. One of the last people I expect to see is running toward us. Logan. I move behind Jess and hope that he doesn't recognize her and doesn't see me.

"Jess!"

No such luck. She slows down and eventually stops. Logan does the same and before I know it, he is blocking the sidewalk and there's no way to avoid talking to him.

"Amy, I didn't even see you. Were you trying to hide behind Jess?"

Yes I was. I wasn't about to admit it to either of them though.

"Hey," I say.

He smiles at us.

"So, I haven't seen you ladies around, where have you been hiding?"

I glance at Jess, hoping that she doesn't say anything, but her attention is on Logan.

"Oh, we've just been around," I say, speaking before Jess can.

Logan turns to me and our eyes lock. I suddenly feel lost, like I'm drifting through space. It's a wonderful feeling that I never want to end. I notice that his mouth is moving, but I don't hear him saying anything.

An elbow in my ribs brings me right back down to Earth.

"What?" I say.

They both laugh and my face turns red. I wish I would have been listening.

"What's so funny?"

"You looked miles away," he says.

"Uh… yeah… sorry, I was thinking about work."

That's the best you can do? You could have said anything.

"Where do you work?"

Before I can even open my mouth, Jess jumps in and answers.

"She works at Burgers-R-Us. It's just like a mile from here."

"Yeah, I know of it, but I've never been there. Is it any good?"

"It's alright I guess."

Logan looks down at his watch.

"I better get back to my run, I've gotta go get ready."

"Yeah, we need to get home, too," Jess says.

Logan steps around me, smiles at us and starts to run. I look over at Jess and she has a huge grin on her face.

"What?"

She starts to laugh and then runs off. I run after her, doing my best to keep up. She picks up the pace as we loop back around and head for the house and it takes everything I have to stay with her.

By the time we get back, I can barely breathe and Jess seems like she's just started to break a sweat.

"That was a great run!" she says.

She turns around and looks at me. I'm bent over with my hands on my thighs, trying desperately to catch my breath.

"Aww, come on, you aren't that out of shape are

you?"

I open my mouth, but I can't speak. I'm too busy still gasping for air. Jess starts to do her post run stretches and I join her when she's about halfway through, and I can finally breathe again.

"Why did you tell him where I work?"

Jess grabs her left ankle and pulls it toward her butt, trying to stretch her leg out as best she can.

"Did you not want me to tell him?"

I'm not sure actually. I don't know why Logan knowing where I work really makes a difference. I'm actually not sure why I even reacted at all to it.

"I don't know, I guess I just don't want him to stop by when I'm working."

Jess finishes stretching and climbs the steps. I follow her inside and we both head for the kitchen to get a drink of water.

"Why not?"

"I guess… I'm not sure really. I can't really explain it."

She pulls out one of the chairs from the dining room table and I sit across from her.

"I mean, be realistic, Amy. He might show up at your work and he might not. If he shows up, fine. Make him order some food and make sure he gives you a good tip. That's all there is to it."

I guess she had a point. It wouldn't hurt for him to come into my work and I definitely could use the money.

"You're right."

"Of course I am."

We both laugh. I'm so glad that I met her, it's been a great week and I'm really looking forward to spending more time with her. I know now that she's going to be a good friend of mine for a long time.

It feels good to have someone in my life right now that I really trust and who seemingly gets me. Especially after everything that's happened with Mitch.

"You OK?"

"What? Yeah, why?"

"Oh, you seemed totally fine and then all of a sudden, you looked really sad," she says.

"Yeah… I'm alright. I was just thinking about Mitch."

I get up and get another glass of water. I stand at the sink and drink it. I'm not sure what to do. I still haven't heard anything from Mitch. For some reason I feel like he will come to his senses and beg me to take him back.

"I just don't know what to do, you know? I invested so much time and energy into my relationship with Mitch, that I feel like it was a total waste the way that it ended. Does that make sense?"

I sit back down at the table. Jess thinks for a minute before she answers.

"I know how you feel. I hate to be the bearer of bad news though, this won't be the last time that a guy breaks your heart or treats you like crap. Finding the guy who you are really supposed to spend your life with isn't easy and you may never meet him. That's the reality of life."

"But why?"

I don't know why I just said that. What a stupid thing to say. I know that life isn't always easy, I guess that I'm just frustrated.

"Because life's a beach and then you fry."

I crack a smile.

"But seriously, you just need to not worry about Mitch. Don't blame yourself for what happened, that's all on him. He wasn't able to see past what everyone else saw and see that you are good and honest and would never hurt him."

She's right. I really didn't do anything wrong. Yes, I admit that maybe I shouldn't have gone out to dinner with Logan, but considering what was happening, with my dad, I think that I deserve the benefit of the doubt.

If Mitch isn't able to give me that, then it's not my fault that he doesn't want to be with me. He will always wonder what he missed out on.

"I say good riddance, you're awesome, Amy. It's his fault for not seeing that."

I hear what she's saying, but my brain can't quite make sense of it. Six months ago, a year ago, yeah I would have agreed with her… but after everything… I just don't know if I believe it anymore and that makes me sad.

"You're right."

I force myself to smile. I'm not going to bring her down with my crap.

"We went over this once already, of course I'm right. I'm always right."

This time when I smile at her it's genuine. She's ridiculous.

"Plus, when you do decide to get back on the wagon, there's someone who I'm sure would be more than happy to help you forget about Mitch."

"I… I don't know what you mean."

"You know exactly what I'm talking about."

We both know she's talking about Logan, but there's no way I would admit that he even crossed my mind. I can feel my face turning bright red.

"I have to get ready for work."

I stand up from the table and start walking to the bathroom. I can hear Jess giggling as the close the door behind myself. I take a deep breath, and run myself a cool shower.

CHAPTER SEVENTEEN

I've only been at work for forty minutes and it already seems like a lifetime. Gary is gone already, heading back to the hospital to visit his mom. I didn't ask how she was doing. I could see it on his face that she wasn't doing well.

The restaurant is still empty so I sit down on the stool in the service area and pull out my phone. I open my phone and see that I have a missed text. My heart skips a beat and then I see that it's not from Mitch, it's from Jess.

Hey, did Logan show up at your work yet?

I almost laugh out loud.

No, and I don't think that he will.

A part of me kind of does want him to come in, for no other reason that it's been so slow that I'm bored and I'm not making any money.

I flip through my phone, still surprised that I haven't heard from my dad again. I sort of expected that he would leave me alone for a couple of days and then try to get in contact with me again.

I guess it's good that he hasn't texted me again since I really have no desire to talk to him, not yet at least. I'm sure that as time passes I will probably get in touch with him. I don't know when it will be though and I'm certainly not in that sort of space yet.

My phone vibrates as I get a response from Jess.

He will show up sometime within the next week. Guaranteed.

You really think so?

Texting Jess has been a godsend. It helps to pass the time between customers and she is always quick to respond since she's at home during the day, at least until classes start in the fall.

Heck yeah. I could tell by the look on his face when I told him where you worked. He was trying to figure out when he could go to your work.

I hadn't noticed, but Jess seems to be pretty good at reading people's faces. A warm feeling passes through my body, similar to what I felt when Logan touched me the first time we met.

The door chimes and I look up. My jaw almost drops when I see Logan walk through the door. He steps inside and looks around. He makes eye contact with me and smiles. I quickly type a message to Jess as he walks toward me.

He's here!

I hit send and push my phone into my pocket. I stand up, grab a menu and walk toward Logan.

"Hey, how are you?"

"Good, how about you?"

"Just working. Did you want to get something to eat?"

He smiles at me and nods. Of course he does, he's in a restaurant. Now he probably thinks I'm an idiot, among other things.

I lead him to a table by the window and I put the menu in front of him as he sits down.

"I'll be right back with your water."

I feel my phone vibrate in my pocket as I walk to the service station. I pull it out and read the text from Jess.

OMG. As soon as he leaves you have to tell me everything.

I put my phone back in my pocket, not wanting to respond and take even longer getting his water and head back to his table. I put his water down and pull out my order pad.

"Do you know what you'd like?"

"You."

"What?"

"Yes, I know what I would like."

I could have sworn he said 'you' the first time I asked him, but I wasn't about to ask him and make myself look silly. There's no way he would have said that. It must just be my mind playing tricks on me.

"Can I get a chicken salad, no dressing, please?"

"Of course."

I write down the order, not because I will forget, but Dan insists that he will forget what he's making, even if there's only one thing on one order. It seems strange to me, but I'm not going to argue.

"And just water to drink."

"I'll be back in a few minutes with your salad."

I walk away before I can make a fool of myself. I've never been clumsy or spastic, but for some reason, whenever I'm around Logan, I feel like I can't speak or walk. It's the weirdest thing.

I hand the order to Dan and go back to the service station and take out my phone to text Jess.

He just sat down and he ordered a chicken salad.

I get a text back almost instantly.

Don't text me, go talk to him! You can tell me later. And I don't need to know what he's eating, that's not what I meant by telling me everything.

I steal a glance at Logan. He's just sitting at the table, sipping on his water and looking at something on his phone. I put my phone away and wait for his salad to be ready. Dan rings the bell and I head to the kitchen.

"No dressing? None at all?"

"No, he didn't want any," I say, shrugging.

"Well, that's boring. It's ready then."

He hands me the plate and after a quick glance at the salad, I agree with Dan, it does look really bland and boring. I bring the salad to Logan and set it down. I glance at his phone, out of curiosity, and it just looks like a bunch of lines and arrows. It must be some game or something.

"What are you playing?"

"Huh?"

"I… I saw your phone. Are you playing a game or something?"

"Oh, no… I was looking at my playbook, for football. We have a new offensive coordinator this year, so I'm still trying to learn the plays and I'm starting to run out of time."

"Oh…"

"Yeah," he says, smiling at me, "I'm sure that it's not all that interesting to you."

"I don't really know that much about football."

"I thought that your boyfriend played?"

As soon as the words leave his mouth, I can see the shift in his face.

"God, I'm… I'm sorry," he says.

I shrug. He didn't mean anything by it, he was just trying to have a conversation and to be fair, I was the one who started by asking about what he was doing on his phone.

"Can I get you anything else?"

He shakes his head and looks down at his salad. I walk back to the service area and sit on the stool and try to not cry. Every time I think that I'm doing alright, something, or someone, reminds me of Mitch and then I'm right back where I started. I hate this. I never thought that someone else could have this kind of effect on me.

My mind wanders as I think about how different my life is now than just a few months ago. I thought things would be different. I thought they would turn out according to plan.

I hear the door chime, so I look up and see Logan walking out of the restaurant. I hop off the stool and go after him. By the time I reach the door, he is already driving away. I sigh, standing in the doorway, as I watch his SUV disappear as he takes a left hand turn at the next intersection.

It's my fault that he just left without saying anything. I just know it is. I'm sure that he felt bad about bringing up Mitch. That's not his fault.

I go over to the table he was sitting at. Next to his uneaten salad is a note written on the back of a receipt, with a hundred-dollar bill underneath it.

Amy, I'm sorry that I said what I did. I never meant to upset you, but I can see that I did. I shouldn't have come. I hope that you can forgive me and that we can be friends.

I pick up the note, put it into my pocket and pick up the money. There's no way that he meant to leave so much. He must have just been so out of sorts that he thought he was leaving a ten and accidently left a hundred.

I bring the untouched salad to the kitchen, dump it in the trash and put the dirty plate in the sink.

"I knew he wouldn't like it," Dan says. "That salad really needs some kind of dressing, otherwise it's super bland."

"No, that wasn't it. He… He had to go suddenly. He just left money on the table and ran out of the restaurant."

It was the truth, just not all of the facts. I didn't need to tell Dan what had really happened. He shrugs and goes back to forming raw hamburger into patties.

I head back into the dining room and pull out my phone.

He just left.

I watch a couple walk up to the front of the restaurant, pause briefly to read the menu that's posted on the window, and then walk off. My phone vibrates with her reply.

Yeah? How did it go?

I take a deep breath and let out a long sigh. I don't even know where to start.

I mentioned that I didn't really know much about football and he was surprised given the fact that I dated a football player.

I shouldn't have opened my mouth. I should have just minded my own business and not asked him about what he was doing on his phone.

Yikes.

Yeah. So then I left him alone to eat and he got up and left a couple minutes later, left a note on the table that said he was sorry for upsetting me and he just left, without saying anything.

Why did I even look at his phone? I have a feeling I'll be reliving the whole conversation in my mind for the next few days, wondering what would have happened if I never said anything and just treated him like any other customer.

Well, that's crappy.

I hear Dan coming out of the kitchen and I put my phone back in my pocket before I can reply to her text.

"I can't take it," he says. "It's so freakin slow."

It is slow. I wouldn't normally care, but I could really use the money. Fall tuition, even for the community college, is going to be really expensive.

"I hope that it starts to get busy, soon."

"It might not until the week before school. Then you're going to be so swamped with tables that you 're going to wish for these slow days where we just stand around."

I had a feeling he was right, but at least when it's busy I'll actually make some money. If not, my birthday is only a month away and I'm sure Jess could probably get me a job at her work. I would almost rather work nights, anyway, I'm not sure how flexible my schedule at school is going to be.

I turn to Dan, but he's gone. I pull out my phone again and there's a text from Jess.

Don't worry, things will work out, they always do.

I wanted to believe her. I just… I don't know sometimes. I feel like right now the only good thing I have going for me is my friendship with her.

Oh, and Logan left a hundred on the table to pay for his salad, so I'm going to have to try and figure out a way to get him his change. Maybe you can help me with that.

Keep it, that's yours. He wouldn't have left it if he didn't want you to have it. He probably felt bad and was trying to make it up to you.

I don't feel like it's right for me to keep it. I can't imagine if I gave someone a hundred instead of a ten, I would be beside myself. I'm going to have to try and give it back to him and if Jess is right, and he did mean to leave me that big of a tip, then he will say that. I can't just keep it though, I feel guilty already and it's only been ten minutes.

CHAPTER EIGHTEEN

"You want some water?"

"Please."

Jess hands me a glass and then fills up her own. We sit down at the kitchen table, in what have become our normal spots, and try to cool ourselves down.

"I can't believe how hot it's getting during our runs, it's ridiculous," I say.

Jess nods and finishes her glass of water and gets up to refill it.

"I know, but it's probably only going to get worse."

I groan. Today was the hottest day yet and I felt like I was being cooked alive as we ran.

"We could always start earlier," she says.

I glare at her and she laughs. We both know that that's never going to happen.

"Or we could just not run."

"We have to keep running," she says. "Don't forget, you're the one that wants to try and return that money to Logan, and unless you want to go to the football housing, the only shot you have at seeing him randomly is during our run."

It's been four days since Logan came into my work and I can't stop thinking about what happened. I'm sure it doesn't help that I have the change from his meal sitting in the outside pouch of my wallet. It's a constant reminder of him, and that day.

"I know."

"Plus, after another couple weeks of this heat and you won't even notice it anymore and then we can start to run four miles."

"Ugh."

She laughs. I'm sure she thinks it's funny to torture me.

"What are you doing tonight?"

I get up and put my glass in the dishwasher.

"Nothing, what I do every night."

She grins at me. It's funny because it's true.

"Alright, well I don't have to work, so you should come with me to this party."

"I dunno, I won't know anyone there."

She waves off my attempt to get out of going to the party.

"You know me. It'll be fun, it's at the house of one of my regulars. He's really fun and he's really cute."

Jess winks at me and I roll my eyes.

"What?" she says.

"Oh, nothing. I have to get ready for work."

"You're going with me."

I close the bathroom door. I haven't been to a party since… since Mitch's graduation and that was a let down. I have no desire to be around a bunch of people I don't know at some strange guy's house.

I already know that no matter how much I don't want to go, Jess is going to find a way to convince me to go with her.

~~~~

"Amy, come on, I know you want to go."

Here we go. I know that despite the fact that I'm tired, thanks to my morning run and the fact that work was sort of busy, that she is going to get me to go somehow. I might as well make her work for it.

"I'm really tired, maybe some other time."

She comes out of her room and into the living room. My eyes grow wide when I see her outfit. Jess has on a deep purple spaghetti strap dress, that leaves little to the imagination and ends barely halfway down her thighs and she's wearing black pumps.

"What? Why are you looking at me like that?"

"Umm."

"Does it look that bad?"

"No, it doesn't look bad… it's just… a little risqué for my tastes."

She flashes me a devious grin.

"Well," she says. "I guess you have to come and be my party buddy, then."

"Your party buddy? What's that?"

She heads into the bathroom and starts to put on eyeliner.

"You know, a party buddy. We keep an eye on each other so that neither of us does something stupid."

That's a new one. She's doing her best to guilt me into going with her.

"Can't someone else be your party buddy?"

"No way, I need you. You seem like the responsible type. Well, more responsible than any of my other friends."

"Fine, I'll go with you and be your party buddy."

"Eeeee!"

She squeals with delight, rushes over to me, grabs my hand, pulling me off the couch and takes me into her room.

"I'm assuming, based on what clothes I've seen you wear that you don't have any party clothes."

"Uh… I was just going to wear jeans and a T-shirt, or something."

Jess puts her hand on her hip and shakes her head in a disapproving manner.

"No."

"No?"

"No."

I sigh. I guess I have no say in the matter. The quicker I relent, the sooner this will all be over.

"Fine. I guess I have no *party clothes*."

She turns to her closet and proceeds to look through everything. I almost want to shut my eyes and just put on whatever she ends up picking out. Maybe if I don't see myself wearing it, it will be like it never happened.

"Perfect!"

"No."

"Yes."

I shake my head. There's no way I'm wearing *that*.

Jess holds up a black tube top dress that has flared bottom. The material looks almost sheer and there's no way that it will even go halfway down my thigh.

"I can't wear that in public… It looks like lingerie."

Jess starts to laugh, but she takes it off the hanger and sets it on the bed, before going to her shoe rack.

"What size do you wear?"

"Seven."

"Amazing."

Jess pulls a pair of gold peep toe pumps off the rack and holds them up.

"What do you think?"

"They are gorgeous, but there's no way that I'm wearing that *dress*."

Jess frowns and puts her free hand on her hip.

"Please?"

I shake my head. There's no way I can wear that. It probably wouldn't even look good on me.

"Do you like the shoes?"

"Yeah, they are beautiful."

"They cost six hundred dollars."

My heart definitely skipped a beat. I can't even fathom spending that much money on a pair of shoes. Heck, all of my clothes put together cost as much as that one pair of shoes.

But they are perfect.

Jess sets the shoes down on the bed next to the dress.

"I'll make you a deal, party buddy."

I don't like where this is going.

"I'm not wearing the dress, Jess, it's out of the question."

"I'll let you keep the shoes, but you have to wear the dress and go to the party with me."

Crap.

Jess starts to giggle. She knows that she has me. I really don't know what to do. I don't really have anything that I could wear with the shoes… But they are so shiny and pretty. I'm sure that I could find something to go with them.

I just really don't know. Is it worth it? I do want the shoes, plus Jess seems like she really wants me to go with her and after everything that she's done for me, I feel like it would only be right for me to go with her. And those shoes.

"Fine, I'll go."

She squeals with delight, hands me the shoes and then the dress. I take them and head to my room.

I set the dress on my bed, step back and take a deep breath. I can't believe I just agreed to this. I'm actually glad that I'm going to a party where I won't know anyone, because this dress is not like anything I would ever normally wear.

I take off my work pants, shirt and shoes and slip the dress on. It fits perfectly, isn't that big of a surprise since we are about the same size. The material actually feels amazing on my skin, it's so soft and light. I slip my feet into the shoes. I can't believe how perfectly they fit and they are actually really comfy. I look down and wiggle my toes. I can't even remember the last time I put any polish on my toes and they look so plain.

"You have any nail polish?"

I hear Jess walk into the room behind me.

"Jesus."

"What?"

I turn around and face her. She looks surprised, her mouth slightly open as he looks me up and down.

"How do I look?"

"You look hot."

I blush. I would never describe myself as hot and it feels good to hear it from someone else, even if it's Jess. I smile at her.

"Do you have any nail polish though? My toes look awful."

She looks down and shrugs.

"They aren't that bad, but I do have some polish. Let me grab it."

I sit down on my bed and pull the shoes off. I glance at my clock, it's eight. I wonder if I have time to paint my toes before we have to be at the party. I don't want to risk putting my shoes on if my toes are wet.

"Do we have time for me to paint my toes?"

I can hear Jess rummaging through stuff in the bathroom.

"Yeah, it's way early to show up at a party. Ah, found it!"

She comes back into my room and hands me a bottle of purple polish that has little sparkles in it. It's dark enough that at night it should go with my dress.

"Cute."

"It's the same color I have on."

I sit down on my bed and put my right foot up on the window sill and shake the polish. Jess goes back to the bathroom and keeps putting on makeup. I finish my right foot and wait for it to dry a little before I put it on the floor and put my left up.

I hear my cell chirp as it announces the arrival of a text. I forgot my phone in the living room and I can't walk yet.

"Jess?"

"Yeah?"

She pops her head into my room.

"Ooh, your toes look cute."

"Thanks. Do you mind grabbing my phone? I think it's in the living room."

"Sure."

I hear it chirp a second time. Jess comes into my room and hands me my phone.

"Sorry, I didn't mean to look, but I was picking it up and a text flashed across the screen that said it was from your Dad."

"Don't worry about it."

I smile at her, so that she knows that it's OK, but at the same time I feel a knot forming in my stomach. Why is he texting me now? Jess smiles at me and leaves my room.

"Should we go in like thirty minutes? The party isn't too far away."

"Yeah, sure, whatever," I say, already distracted by the texts I haven't opened yet.

I take a deep breath and slide my finger across the screen of my phone to unlock it and open the texts.

Amy, I know that things haven't been that good between us, lately, but I really want to see you. I have an early birthday present for you that I figured I could give you now and I also have some other good news that I wanted to share with you. I love you.

The last part makes me cringe. Does he really? I

know he loves me in the sense that I'm his daughter, but does his love run any deeper than obligation? I admit that I'm a little curious as to what the good news could possibly be. I just don't know if talking to him is worth it to find out, it could be nothing, really. I read the next text.

Please just call me or text me back. Love you.

There are those words again. I take a deep breath. I set my phone down on my bed. I can't deal with right now. I check to see if my toes are dry yet. They seem like it, so I head into the bathroom where Jess is just finishing up her makeup.

"Is everything OK?"

"Oh, yeah, it's whatever. He just wanted to talk to me."

"Do you want to call him? We can wait to leave if you want to?"

"No, it's alright, I'm still not sure if I even want to talk to him. Not yet at least."

"Just don't let too much time go by, you never know what can happen in life."

I nod. I know she's right and I will need to talk to him eventually, even if I don't think he deserves it. It can wait though, I'm not going to let him make me feel guilty. Not after how he acted.

"You're right. I just need a little more time before I'm ready to talk to him."

CHAPTER NINETEEN

"So, did you say that this guy is a customer of yours?"

I close the door and buckle my seatbelt. Jess does the same and starts the car.

"Yeah, he's a regular and he tips really well."

"Have you been to one of his parties before?"

She starts the car and backs out of the driveway. We head down the road in the direction of the football housing.

"Yeah, just once. It was crazy."

I'm only sort of listening as we drive by the building and I find myself looking to see if Mitch's truck is there. I don't see it, but I do see Logan's SUV. I force myself not to think either of them and turn my attention back to Jess.

"Oh, yeah?"

"Yeah, it was a little nuts. I don't really remember much about that night, but I will never forget the headache that I woke up with the next day."

Wow. I can't even imagine.

"Crazy."

"Yeah, it was a lot of fun though. I've been hounding him to throw another party since then and he finally did."

I'm not sure why she is in such a hurry to repeat that experience. It doesn't sound all that fun to me.

"Is he a student?"

She shakes her head and turns the car to the left, going down a street I've never seen or heard of before.

"No, I think he graduated a couple of years ago, but I'm not sure. He's some sort of business guy, I don't really know. He tried to explain it to me once, but it sounded really boring."

We both laugh. Jess slows the car down and starts to look for a parking spot. I guess we must be getting close because there are cars lining both sides of the road and people walking on the sidewalk.

Jess parks the car in the first open spot she sees and we get out. I'm about to ask how far of a walk it is to the party, because frankly I barely made it to the car in these shoes, but I can hear the music blaring from just down the street.

I feel strange, as we start to walk, not having my purse or phone with me, but Jess said that I should leave them both at the house so I didn't have to worry about keeping track of them during the party. I have a feeling that she thinks I'm going to cut loose in an attempt to forget everything that's happened recently.

That's never going to happen. Yes, of course I would like to forget all the crap that's happened, but I know that it would just be temporary and then tomorrow, when I wake up with a massive hangover, my problems are still going to be there. It's just not worth it, I don't think.

"Are you ready?"

I force a smile and look at Jess, who looks like she's genuinely excited.

"As ready as I'll ever be."

She wraps her arm through mine and we step off the sidewalk and onto the path that leads to the house. I try to stop and gawk at the house, but Jess pulls on my arm. The house has a large wooden double door that looks like it belongs on an old church. There are large bay windows on the ground floor and I can see outlines of people dancing behind the curtains. The windows on the second floor are no less impressive, but slightly smaller. There are lights, every few feet, around the exterior of the house, that are facing up and illuminating the bright orange paint. It's not a color I've ever seen a house painted, but it looks amazing.

A young couple in front of us holds the door open and we head inside. Crammed into every nook and cranny of the living room are people, huddled close and trying to talk above the constant thumping of the music. In the center of the room a group of girls who look to be our age are dancing.

I follow Jess into the kitchen, which takes some time as we wade through the crowd. Plus she has to stop every few feet to talk to someone she knows, from work I guess.

Her eyes light up as she steps up to the counter, which has more alcohol than I've ever seen in my life. She grabs a red cup and starts to mix. I quickly lose track of what's going in the cup as I watch her work. It's amazing.

Jess turns to me and holds out the drink. I shake my head and hold up my hands.

"I'm good, but thank you."

She frowns at me, lifts the drink to her lips and takes a sip.

"You sure? It's really good."

"I'm sure."

"You don't even want to take one baby sip?"

"Maybe later."

She wrinkles her nose at me and smiles and then takes another drink, much longer this time.

"Mmmm."

She says it loud enough so that I can hear. I just smile at her and shake my head. She's ridiculous. I have a feeling that this whole 'party buddy' thing is more for her benefit than mine and that's just fine with me.

A guy walks up to Jess and gives her a kiss on the cheek, which she returns. He looks to be in his early thirties and he's fairly good looking. Jess turns to me.

"This is Rick. This is his house."

I nod and hold out my hand, but he leans forward, wraps his arms around me and gives me a kiss on the cheek as he hugs me. I stand there, not knowing what to do really.

"Nice to meet you," I say, once he releases me and steps back. "I'm Amy."

"The pleasure is all mine."

He leans into Jess and whispers something into her ear and she nods in response. He smiles at me before leaving the room.

"He seems nice," I say.

"What?"

I step closer to her and lean my head close to her ear so that I don't have to yell.

"He seems nice."

"Yeah he is, plus he's really cute, don't you think?"

"Sure."

He is kind of cute, I guess, but he seems a little old. I mean, he's not old in terms of how long people generally live, but he's probably fifteen years older than us.

Jess finishes her drink and goes back to the counter to make another. I almost want to tell her to be careful, to slow down and take it easy and I don't. I guess I'll be driving us home tonight.

She turns back to me, this time with a cup in each hand. She holds the one in her right hand out to me. I shake my head and mouth 'No' to her, but she only pushes it closer to me. I take the cup to humor her, but I have no intention of drinking it.

Jess looks past me. I turn around to see what she's

looking at, and I see Logan, walking through the front door of the house. I spin back to face Jess. She has a huge grin on her face and she lifts her drink to cover it up.

I start to panic. Even though I did want to see him, to give him back his money, I didn't want to see him *here*, when I'm wearing *this*. I can feel my heart racing. I do the only thing I can think of. I lift the cup to my lips and let the alcohol slide down my throat. It goes down way too easy. Maybe Jess didn't give me any alcohol and just wanted me to embrace the idea of having a drink. Whatever she gave me, tasted kind of like a really lemony iced tea.

"Here's your chance, he's heading our way."

I glance over my shoulder and see Logan heading toward the kitchen, but he's talking to someone and doesn't see me. At least I don't think he does.

I hand my cup to Jess and dash out of the kitchen. There are two ways out, in addition to the way that Logan is coming, and I choose the open French doors that lead to the deck. There are people on the deck too, and even a few people in the hot tub and swimming pool. I follow the deck as it wraps around the side of the house.

A look at the back door makes me feel a little better. I don't see Logan, so that means he didn't see me. I know that it's possible that he might talk to Jess and she could tell him where I went, but he would still have to wander around in the mostly dark backyard to try and find me.

I feel a sudden urge to fall over. I really need to sit down. I turn around, slowly, and see an outdoor couch against the house. I walk over to it and sit. I wonder why I feel so dizzy all of a sudden.

After a few minutes I start to feel bored, and lonely, since I have no one to talk to. I'm not about to go back inside though, not as long as Logan might be in there. I look down at myself. It's still hard to believe that I let Jess talk me into wearing this dress tonight.

I watch as a couple walks into the darkest corner of the deck, with their drinks in hand, and starts to make out. I turn away, not wanting them to catch me watching.

As I look back to the side of the deck where I came from, I feel the couch move slightly. The couple that had just been making out in the corner are now sitting on the other end of the couch and seem to be inching their way closer to me with each passing moment.

I jump up from the couch, take a moment to make sure I don't fall over as I realize I'm even more dizzy now, and I walk back toward the rear of the house. When I get to the corner, I peek around it. I don't see Logan, so I look for my next place to sit down. I see a lawn chair, near the hot tub and pool, and I make my way toward it.

I barely make it to the chair, but I do, and when I sit down it's the best feeling in the world. The world spins for a few more seconds and then slows down. I take a deep breath and find myself people watching.

There's a few people in the pool, just swimming around and splashing water on each other, there's two girls and a guy sitting in the hot tub and a few small groups of people milling around the yard.

I avert my eyes as the two girls in the hot tub start kissing the guy at the same time. That's a little more than I need to see. Instead, I find myself looking directly at a guy's crotch. I close my eyes and turn my head, again.

"It's not that bad of a view."

It's Logan's voice. I open my eyes and glance back in the direction of the crotch. Logan is squatting next to me and in each hand he has a drink. He holds one out and before he can say anything I grab it out of his hand and start guzzling it.

It tastes just like the drink Jess gave me. Dang you, Jess. She must have told him where I went and gave him a drink to give to me. I finish the drink and hand the cup back to Logan. His eyes go wide.

I realize, as I look at Logan, that the drinks Jess

made for me do in fact have alcohol, but she disguised the taste quite well. It tastes nothing like the one other time in my life I had a drink, but that was just a sip and it was straight whiskey. Whatever she made me is dangerous and I instantly regret drinking them.

"Hi," he says.

"Hi."

"How are you?"

"Fine," I say, shrugging.

"You look very pretty tonight."

I totally forgot what I was wearing. My face turns bright red. Hopefully it's dark enough out here that he doesn't notice.

"Thanks."

"So, how have you been?"

"I forgot my purse."

"OK, do you need if for something?"

I nod. I feel like it's getting harder to speak with each passing moment. The words that form in my head are nothing like what is coming out of my mouth.

"Where is your purse?"

Logan stands up and starts to look around.

"No. Not here, it's at home."

"What do you need it for?"

"Money, for you."

He looks at me with a confused look on his face.

"You left me too much, I want to give it back."

He suddenly understands what I'm getting at and he flashes me that smile of his. That beautiful, warming smile. I feel like I'm about to melt. Logan squats back down and I catch a whiff of him. He smells amazing. I didn't think boys could smell this good.

"I meant to leave you that much. I felt really bad about what I said and I felt like it would be a nice gesture for someone who's going through a rough time in their life."

What does that mean? He's giving me money

because he feels bad for me? I don't need his pity or his money. I need to get out of here. At the very least I need to get away from him.

I stand up too quickly and fall forward. I close my eyes and tense my body as I get ready to land on my face. I feel big hands grab me around the waist and lower me back down onto the chair. I can't believe he caught me so easily.

"I think you should just sit here for a couple minutes."

"Where's Jess? I want to go home."

"I'll go find her."

I watch as Logan goes back inside. I hope that he can find her. I don't want to be here anymore. I can't believe Logan, what a jerk. I'm not some charity case.

The world starts to spin and I close my eyes, which helps some, but I still feel dizzy and I feel like I'm about to throw up.

"Amy?"

I open my eyes and the spinning gets faster. I cover my mouth and try not to throw up, but it doesn't help. I cover Logan's shoes and the bottom of his pants in whatever food was still in my stomach from dinner.

I close my eyes and start to cry.

"I want to go home."

Logan puts one arm under my knees and his other under my neck and lifts me off the chair, as if I weigh nothing. He carries me down the steps of the deck and around to the side of the house.

"Where are you taking me?"

"I'm taking you home."

He carries me to his SUV, sets me down just long enough to open the passenger door and lifts me up and puts me in the seat. He leans across me, his face an inch from mine as he buckles my seatbelt and I smell it again. That wondrous smell. My body is telling me to reach out and touch him, but my mind is telling me that I should be furious at him right now, for how he decided that I needed a handout.

Logan closes the passenger door, climbs into the driver's side of the SUV and starts it. I close my eyes as he starts to drive. The motion is a little much for me and even though I'm mad at him right now, I don't want to throw up in here.

When I open my eyes again he is pulling his SUV into my driveway. I have no idea how he knows where I live, but I don't care right now. I just want to go to bed. As I struggle with the seat belt, Logan jumps out and opens my door and tries to help me.

"I don't need your help, I got it."

He stands back and lets me try to take off the seat belt. I give up and throw my head against the headrest as tears start to flow from my eyes. I do need help, I just don't want to admit it. And I don't really want help from him.

"Just let me help you."

He takes my lack of an answer as a 'yes' and reaches across me, unbuckles the seatbelt and helps me out. I lean against him all the way to the front door and finally let go, fairly confident that I can make it the rest of the way. I instantly fall and Logan catches me, for the second time.

"Where's your key?"

"Under the mat."

Logan lifts the mat and grabs the spare key, while managing to keep me from falling over. He unlocks the door and helps me inside. I brace myself with him and we walk to my bedroom. I pull myself free of Logan and fall, face first, into bed.

I feel Logan's hand on my ankle, and I don't react, I just don't have the energy to do or say anything, and he slips my shoe off. He does the other one and then puts his hands on my shoulders and rolls me on my side.

"You can't sleep face down or face up."

I don't know what he's talking about, but I'm in no shape to protest. I try to sit up, but the room starts to spin as soon as I move. I close my eyes and try not to think about how mad I am at Logan.

"Are you OK?"

I open my eyes for a brief moment and see Logan sitting on the floor next to my bed.

"I'm so mad at you."

"I know," he says.

"Do you know why?"

"Yes. You're mad because I left you a good tip at work."

"I don't need your money."

I feel like I might have to throw up again, but I force it back down. Ugh, gross.

"I know you don't. I just thought that since it seemed so slow and I know you moved and you could probably use the money. You're trying to read too much into it, Amy. I was just trying to be nice."

"Is that all?"

Logan pauses. I open my eyes and look at him. He looks me in the eyes and I feel like he knows me, that he gets me. I don't know why I've been so standoffish with him. It's like for the first time, I met someone who really knows me and gets me and I keep trying to push him away. Stupid.

"I really like you," he says.

"I like you, too."

"Amy," he says. "I really like you and I hope that in time you will give me a chance to be more than just your friend."

My body feels different as his words wash over me. I've been trying to convince myself, since the first moment I saw Logan, that he was wrong for me. I don't know why I didn't just listen.

"Kiss me."

"Amy, I don't know if that's a good idea."

169

"Kiss me."

Logan leans forward and presses his lips against mine. His tongue darts into my mouth and I can feel heat passing through my whole body. It's unlike anything I've ever felt before and I never want it to end.

He breaks the kiss and smiles at me.

"As much as I enjoyed that, you really need to brush your teeth."

Oh god. I completely forgot that I threw up earlier, on Logan no less, and then I insisted he kiss me. He must be so freaked out and disgusted with me right now. Before I can apologize for that awful tasting kiss, I hear my phone ringing from the living room. Who would be calling me at this time of night?

CHAPTER TWENTY

"Do you want me to get that?" Logan says.

I shake my head. Whoever is calling can leave a message. I just want to sit here and stare into his eyes until I drift into sleep.

"It's fine, they can leave a message."

His body relaxes again once the ringing ceases.

"I'm sorry," I say.

"About what?"

"Hopefully this makes sense and I'm not babbling. I'm not quite myself right now. I'm sorry that I've been so cold to you, tonight and since we met. You're amazing and I feel bad about how I've acted toward you."

"Oh, I thought you were going to apologize for the puke kiss."

I can tell by the playful tone that he was teasing me, but I still can't believe I did that.

My phone starts to ring again. Logan jumps up and is halfway to the door before I can say anything.

"Don't worry about answering it."

"It's the Salem Police Department."

I hope that Jess is safe and that nothing happened to her. I don't have any idea why they would be calling my cell or how they would even have my number.

"Answer it, just in case," I say.

"Hello?"

I can hear Logan walking back to the bedroom.

"Yeah, this is her phone."

He stops halfway into the room and looks at me. The look on his face is one of sadness and compassion. I jump out of bed and rush to him, ignoring the toll the alcohol has taken on my body.

"Is it Jess?"

He shakes his head and holds out the phone to me. Why else would they be calling me and what could they have said to Logan for him to look at me the way he did.

"Hello?"

"Amy?"

"Yes."

"My name is Officer Jim Tulley and I need to talk to you for a moment, it's about your dad."

I can hear it in his voice. He doesn't have to say the words, I already know. I look at Logan. His eyes say how sorry he is.

"Are you there?"

"Yes," I say, my voice trembling.

"Your father, he was the victim of a carjacking."

"Is he OK?"

I don't know why I ask. I already know.

"I'm so sorry, but by the EMT's made it to him, there was nothing they could do."

The phone falls out of my hands and I feel like I'm about to fall over. I can't breathe or think. Logan wraps his arms around me and walks me over to the bed and helps me sit down.

He picks the phone up off the floor.

"Sorry about that."

I put my head on the pillow and close my eyes. I feel numb.

I hear Logan walk out of the room, still on the phone. I close my eyes as I start to cry. Logan comes back into the room and sits down on the bed next to me and runs his hand through my hair. Each sob sends a quiver through my body as I struggle to breathe. I feel like there's a thousand-pound weight on my chest.

The bed moves as Logan lies down next to me. He kisses the back of my head and wraps his arm over me and holds me tight. I feel like he's the only thing keeping me from falling into an abyss. He can't ever let go or I'll be lost.

Neither of us says anything for the next few minutes. I'm still crying, and he's still holding me, when there's a knock on the door. Logan kisses me on the cheek and gets out of bed.

"That's the Police. They want to talk to you. I can tell them to come back if you want."

I shake my head and take a deep breath. Logan helps me stand up and helps me walk into the living room. I sit down on the couch and he goes to answer the door, letting Officer Tulley in. They come into the living room and sit down, Logan next to me on the couch and Tulley in the chair across from me.

"I'll try to make this quick, I'm sure you want to be alone."

I nod. I still feel like I can't breathe. Is this real? Is he really gone? I can't even imagine never talking to my dad again.

"Did you know your dad was on his way to come see you?"

I shake my head. What was he doing coming here? And how was he going to find me? Logan puts his hand on my leg.

"Well, from what we can gather, it looks like he was on his way here to see you. He stopped at a light, just inside the city limits and was approached by someone, who tried to steal his car, at gunpoint. Your dad resisted and the assailant shot him and ran off."

I put my hands over my face as I cry. Logan wraps his arms around me and pulls me close. He's the only thing keeping me sane right now. I want to scream. What was he thinking? Why would he be here? If he just stayed at home and minded his own business, and didn't try to find me, he would still be alive right now.

"Do you have any questions?"

I have a million questions. I open my mouth, but no matter what I want to say, nothing comes out.

"I'm going to leave you my card, so that you can call me and we can talk another time. You're still in a state of shock, we don't need to do this right now."

Tulley pulls a business card out of his pocket and sets it on the coffee table.

"I also have this for you," Tulley says, setting a folder down on the table. "It is a couple of documents that we found in the car. We've copied them for evidence, and I thought you might like to have these."

He stands up, forces a smile, as he makes eye contact with Logan, and lets himself out of the front door. Logan holds me tighter and puts my head against his chest. He kisses the top of my head and leans his mouth close to my ear.

"I'm here, if you need anything. Anything at all."

"Just hold me," I say, each word a struggle. "And don't let go."

~~~

I wake up a few hours later, my head still on Logan's chest. I can tell by his even breathing that he's asleep. It feels so good to be close to him, to have his arms wrapped around me. Then reality sets it. I remember why we are on the couch and why he's holding me tight.

My dad is dead. Killed by someone who wanted his car. Why didn't he just let them have his car? I start to cry and Logan stirs under me and squeezes his arms tighter around me.

"Are you OK? Can I get you anything."

I can't even bring myself to answer. I feel like my brain is empty, there is just nothingness everywhere and I can't escape it. Nothing feels right. I feel numb. I close my eyes and pray for all of this to disappear.

When I open my eyes, I look at the folder that Officer Tulley left. I want to open it and see what he left that he thought I might want to see, but I just can't do it. It's too much.

"Do you want to see what's in the folder?" Logan says.

He kisses the back of my head again and runs his hand up and down my arm. A calm feeling runs through my body. I don't know what I would do if Logan wasn't here.

Logan lets go of me and I sit back on the couch.

"Can you read it to me?"

He looks at me and our eyes meet. I feel like he can see into the deepest part of my soul. Logan picks up the folder, without looking away from me.

"Are you sure?"

I nod my head. I don't think I could read it, whatever it happens to be. I try to imagine what it could possibly be. What could he have needed to give me so badly that he would drive all the way here without even knowing where I live?

Logan open's the folder and quickly scans a few pieces of paper. One has an official looking letterhead, but I can't quite make it out from where I'm sitting.

"There's a letter here, from State and there's also a personal note here from your dad."

I take a deep breath. I can't imagine why State would be sending me a letter.

"Just tell me what the one from State says."

I'm not ready to listen to his reasoning for coming to see me. It's what got him killed. I feel like I might never understand, no matter what it is. I recall his text where he said he had an early birthday present for me. There's no way he would have come this far just for that.

Logan takes a minute to quickly read the letter.

"They are saying they made a mistake and that you should have been admitted."

What? Did he say what I think he did?

"Wait… what?"

"It's an apology and a retraction on their previous letter."

"Let me see."

He hands it to me and I jump to the first paragraph.

Please forgive our previous oversight. It has come to our attention that during the application entry process, there was a transposition of numbers in high school GPA, which led to an automatic rejection.

I almost can't believe what I'm reading. I skip to the third and final paragraph.

As compensation for this mistake, we would like to offer you a meal plan for your first two semesters at no cost to you. We apologize for any inconvenience that this may have caused you, or your family, and we are looking forward to seeing you this fall. Please contact us if you have any further questions.

I want to scream. I ball up the letter and throw it across the room. Is this for real?

"Are you OK?"

"No… I'm not."

After all I've been through, to find out that State made a mistake is just the icing on the cake. I can't believe that my last few days with my mother, my only parent now, were spent in silence because someone made an error entering my application.

"I got a letter of rejection, which put a serious

strain on my family life when my parents found out. My mom, who ended up leaving my dad a few days later, didn't talk to me and didn't go to my graduation."

"Wow, that's awful."

I nod and shift my body on the couch so that I'm facing Logan. He does the same.

"Yeah... it was bad. Basically, after she left, my dad started drinking and one thing led to the next. Eventually I left home, without telling him where I was going and came here, with Mitch."

Mitch. I wonder if maybe my dad called Mitch and he told him where I was, or at least gave him a general idea. Would he do that? I don't think the old Mitch would have told him anything... but now? There's no other explanation.

"Wow, I'm so sorry, that must have been very hard for you."

I nod. I don't think I can even explain it to Logan. It's something that will stay with me the rest of my life. That's how I felt before... and now, well now I guess that all of this, everything that has happened since my rejection from State will forever change me. I don't know how, but I know that it will.

There's no way that things can ever be the same again.

Logan leans toward me and wraps his arms around me. He doesn't have to say anything. Just our bodies touching reminds me that not everything in this world is bad. There are some things worth living for.

We sit on the couch, not saying a word to each other until the sun comes up. I feel like if I don't move, and we don't get up, then it won't be real.

I hear the door knob turning, and Logan and I both turn our heads. The door slowly swings open and Jess walks in. She doesn't notice us right away, instead closing the door and tiptoeing toward her room.

I clear my throat and she freezes and turns toward

us. She cracks a smile.

"Well, look at you two," she says.

I'm sure that she is amused by walking into the house and seeing me, still in the dress she loaned me, and in the arms of a guy who I tried to avoid at all costs last night.

Under any other circumstances I would have smiled back at her and taken her teasing. But now... I can't even manage to fake a smile.

"You left early, party buddy. Now I see why."

Logan shakes his head and glares at her.

"Is something wrong?" she says.

I wait to see if Logan will say anything, but he's silent. I was hoping that he would tell her what happened, but it's not fair to put that kind of pressure on him. I take a deep breath and try to think about how to explain it to her.

"My dad, he was killed last night."

The look on her face shifts from playful to shock. She slowly walks across the room and sits down in the chair across from the couch. She looks me in the eyes and I have to look away.

"My god, are you alright?"

I don't answer. What am I supposed to say to that? Of course I'm not alright, my dad was just murdered.

"I don't know why I said that," Jess says. "You must be in shock. I can't believe this happened. We just talked about him."

She's right. We talked about him yesterday, and she told me that I needed to talk to him before too much time went by and it was too late. I brushed the idea off and now I'm regretting not answering any of his calls or texts.

I'm starting to feel guilty, as if somehow I'm part to blame for him being killed.

"Do you want to talk about it at all?"

I shake my head. I've been thinking about it for hours already, I would like to think about anything other than my dad.

"Is there anything I can do?" she says.

I try to think about what I have to do. I guess now I will have to go home and deal with his arrangements and then… then I don't know what comes next.

"Maybe you could give me a ride back to Greenville?"

"I can take you, if you want" Logan says.

I push my head into his chest and close my eyes. I can't think about it anymore right now. The thought of having not only lost my dad, but now I have to deal with taking care of whatever comes next, all because my mom is too busy running around Hollywood like a twenty-year-old actress.

"I'm going to leave you two alone. If you need anything, I'll be in my room."

"Thanks," Logan says.

She gets up and walks to her room, closing the door.

I still don't feel like it's real. He's really gone. I'll never speak to him or see him again. I'll never eat his pancakes again.

CHAPTER TWENTY-ONE

"You ready to go?" Logan says.

I look around my room, making sure that I'm not forgetting anything. My clothes are packed in the duffel bags that I brought them here in. I'm not sure how long it will take to do whatever it is I need to do in Greenville.

"I think so... I don't know where my phone is though. Have you seen it?"

Logan shrugs and walks out of my room.

"Found it in the living room."

He comes back into my room and hands me my phone. I turn it on, for the first time in two days. I just felt like I needed to disconnect from the world and be in a quiet space where no one could bother me so I turned it off when Logan left the morning after my dad was killed.

Logan grabs the duffel bags and heads toward the front door. He looks over his shoulder and his lips curl slightly before he goes through the door and toward his SUV, with my bags.

My dad's body was taken back to Greenville yesterday, to Anderson's Mortuary, the only place in town and they are expecting me to stop by tonight so that we can make final preparations for the service, which is tomorrow.

I put my phone in my pocket and head into the living room. Jess gets up from the couch and gives me a hug.

"I don't know how long all of this will take, so I'm not sure when I'll be back."

She breaks the hug, takes a step back and takes my hands in hers.

"Don't worry about it, your room isn't going anywhere. Take all the time you need."

I force myself to smile. She's been so amazing since the day I met her. I can't believe I have to leave right now. I just want to sit around with her and Logan. They are the only things keeping me sane.

"Thank you, you've been amazing."

"Take care of yourself," she says.

"You too."

We hug one last time and I head outside, where Logan is waiting at the passenger door of his SUV. He closes the door and gets in the driver's side.

"You ready?" he says.

"As ready as I'll ever be."

We both look out the passenger window and wave to Jess, who is standing on the porch. She waves back and blows us a kiss. I blow her a kiss back as Logan starts the car and pulls away.

I really hope that I'm not gone for too long, I'm really going to miss her.

"Did you remember to call work?" Logan says.

"Nope, I'll do it right now."

It had totally slipped my mind. I hadn't shown up to work since the day of the party, obviously, but I did want to call Gary and tell him that I won't be coming back, at least for now. He deserves that much after giving me a job. I actually feel a little bad about it, but I can't worry about that.

I take my phone out and my eyes grow wide. I

have thirty new text messages and forty-five new voicemails. Holy crap. My phone was only off for two days. I can deal with those during the ride, but I want to call Gary right away, to get it over with. I pull up the number for Burgers-R-Us and hit call. The phone rings as I put it up to my ear and it's answered between the second and third rings.

"Burgers-R-Us, where we are burgers."

"Gary?"

"Yes, this is Gary speaking."

"Hey, this is Amy."

"Amy, what's going on? I called you repeatedly the last two days. How come you didn't show up for work?"

I take a deep breath. He sounds irritated and I'm sure that once I tell him my reason for not showing up to work, he will understand, but that doesn't make this near verbal assault any easier.

"My dad was killed three nights ago."

I don't say anything else, I feel like that should be enough of an explanation. There's only silence from the other end of the line.

"Was that… was that him on the news? The carjacking?"

"Yes."

"Did they catch the guy?"

"Gary, I need to get off the phone, I'm heading to my hometown to bury my father, I don't have time to get into details."

The reality of the situation was that I didn't know much more than anyone who had watched the news the last couple of days.

"Right, of course."

"I don't know how long I'll be gone, so you should probably just hire someone to replace me."

"Well, thanks for letting me know. Take care and if you do end up back in Salem and want to work, come back in. We can always use a hard working waitress."

"Thanks."

I hang up the phone before he can say anything else. I take a deep breath, turn my phone off and put it in my purse. The texts and voicemails are going to have to wait. I can't deal with them right now.

Logan moves his right hand to my leg and gives it a light squeeze. I take his hand in mine and look over at him and watch him as he drives. He has a certain strength and I know that without him I wouldn't be doing nearly as well. I guess he came into my life when I needed him most.

We drive in silence for a while, Logan's hand resting on my leg and my hand on top of his. I watch him the whole time.

He looks over and our eyes lock for a brief moment. I feel like time slows as we gaze into each other's soul. It's something that I've never felt before. I'm starting to realize that Logan is making me feel a lot of things for the first time.

I smile at him, my first real smile in days. He smiles back and then turns his attention back to the road.

The closer we get to Greenville, and my real home, the worse I start to feel. I know what's there waiting for me, no matter what I do. I'm going to have to face something that I thought would never come. I thought my dad would live forever. Or that he would at least live to be old and pleased with the life he lived. I feel tears starting to form in my eyes, so I look out of the window.

I'm starting to recognize places. We are getting close to Greenville, it's maybe twenty minutes further. I can't imagine sleeping in my bed again, in the house I said goodbye to, without either of my parents there. It's going to be weird. I'm really glad that Logan is here.

"Have you ever been to Greenville?"

"Yeah, just for a football game, so I only really saw a bit of the town and the field at the school."

"Did you win?"

He looks over at me and cracks a smile.

"What?" I say.

"You're cute."

"Why?"

"You just are."

He takes my hand and brings it to his mouth and kisses it. It's the first time his lips have touched my skin since our brief, vomit-filled kiss and I feel a shot of electricity run through my whole body. I shudder as he kisses my hand a second time. He moves our hands back to my leg.

I look at the window as we pass the 'Welcome to Greenville' sign. It's a little ironic, I had a feeling that I would be back here someday, but I never thought that my dad would be the one to get me back to Greenville and now it's the last thing he's done before we say goodbye.

"Where to?"

"Oh, right, sorry. Take the next left, Bunker Street."

He turns down the street where I lived my whole life. I feel a rush of emotions pour through me. I glad to be here in the sense that this is home. At the same time, so much has happened over the last few months and Greenville reminds me of all of it.

"It's that one," I say, pointing at my house.

Logan pulls his SUV into the driveway, turns it off and looks over at me.

"Are you ready?"

"I guess so," I say.

We get out and I try to grab one of the duffel bags, but Logan grabs them both and nods his head toward the house. I fish house keys out of my purse and we climb the back steps. I unlock the door and push it in.

A wave of stale air hits us as we step inside. It smells like stale beer and old food. As we walk through the kitchen and into the living room, I can see why. There are empty beer cans, and bottles, everywhere and empty pizza boxes stacked on the couch and coffee table.

I go up the stairs and Logan follows me, still carrying the duffel bags. When I reach the top, I notice that the door to my parent's room is open, but I'm not ready for that. I pause for a second and turn the knob on my door.

We step into my room. It's exactly how I left it. There's a thin layer of dust coating everything. My dad must have not come in here after I left.

I suddenly feel very sad, not about my dad, but for him. Mom and I both left him and he ended up alone and he died alone. I sit down on my bed and put my head in my hands. Logan drops the bags on the floor and kneels down in front of me and puts his hands on my knees.

"Hey, it's going to be OK. We are going to get through this, I promise."

I want to believe him, and deep down I think I do, but I just don't know what to do. What do I do now? I'm not ready to navigate the rest of my life without my parents. It feels like I was just here, in my room, and they were in the house with me and everything was fine.

"I just feel so lost."

"I know, I get it. I really do. You don't need to worry, I'm here for you. Anything you need, I'm your man."

He lifts himself up and kisses my forehead. I wrap my arms around him and rest my head on his shoulder.

"Thank you."

I notice Logan shifting his weight, trying to not kneel on his left knee anymore and I let go of him and sit up.

"Are you OK?"

"Yeah," he says, trying to hide the twinge of pain that kneeling has caused him.

I pat the bed next to me and he looks relieved to move off the floor. He takes it slow, pushing off the floor and steadying himself.

"Are you sure you're alright?"

He smiles at me as he sits down, puts his arm around my waist and pulls me closer to him.

"I'm fine, it's just an old football injury."

I want to ask him about it, I just don't have the mental energy. We still have so much that we don't know about each other, but I'm not worried. I feel such a strong emotional connection to Logan that I know in time we will come to discover everything about one another.

"Should we go to the mortuary?" I say.

I want to get it over with. The sooner the better.

Logan stares at the wall and nods his head. He seems like he's miles away.

"Yeah," he says, finally turning his attention back to me as he stands.

I glance at the open door that belonged to my parents, again, as we leave my room. It sends a chill down my spine. Logan grabs my hand and holds it as we walk downstairs and to his SUV.

"Go back the way we came."

He nods and pulls out of the driveway. We pass back through town. Everything reminds me of a good memory. I thought that moving away had been all good, but now that I'm back here, I'm starting to remember the good times.

"Turn right here."

Logan takes the turn, and he sees the mortuary on the right and pulls into their modest parking lot. It's not a big place, but large enough for a place like Greenville. I've never actually been, even though I can't even count the number of times I've driven by. Every time I passed it, I hoped that I would never have to walk through the ancient looking doors.

We get out and walk to the door, holding hands. Logan gives me a squeeze. I hope he knows how much it means to me to have him here. A man opens the door as we approach and holds it open, until we are inside, and then he steps around us and holds out his hand. I shake it first.

"Amy?"

I nod my head as he grasps my hand with both of his.

"I'm so sorry for your loss."

"Thank you."

He grasps Logan's hand the same way.

"I'm so sorry for your loss."

Logan just nods.

"I'm Kevin Anderson, we talked on the phone."

I had talked to him when I made the arrangement to have my dad's body moved here.

"Nice to meet you," I say.

"If you would follow me into the office, we can discuss the arrangements."

Logan and I nod and follow him down a hallway and into the second door on the right. Kevin sits behind the small desk and we sit down opposite him.

"I just wanted to say that if any point you need anything, we are here to help you. I know this is a tough time and this isn't easy for someone your age to handle."

"Thanks."

"Now, as we discussed, you don't want to do a formal ceremony here at our chapel, correct?"

I shake my head. I don't know if it's what my dad had wanted, but the thought of it is more than I can handle. I can't imagine having to speak to everyone in town and explain to them that I didn't know why he came to see me. I would have to look each of them in the eyes as they judged me for moving, as if his death was my fault.

"So, you want to just have a burial in the cemetery, with no reception?"

"Yes."

"You understand that this isn't particularly… conventional."

I nod. My family was never that religious and we only went to church on holidays. I don't know what my dad would have wanted, but this is the best I can do. I can't do a full on service, it's just too much.

"Does eleven, tomorrow morning, work for you?"

"That's fine."

Kevin makes a notation on one of the papers that are spread out in front of him on the desk.

"Alright. So, usually for this type of service, we would have Pastor Evans present to do the ceremony. Is that alright?"

I've never met Pastor Evans, but I know that he's the priest at First Disciples, which is the only church in town.

"That's fine."

"Would you like him to say a prayer?"

"Whatever you think."

I'm trying to make as few decisions as possible. Logan reaches over and takes my hand and gives it a light squeeze.

Kevin makes a few notes, this time on a different piece of paper. His eyes quickly scan the rest of the papers, making sure that he hasn't missed anything.

"Well, I think that's it. I have your phone number if I have any last minute questions."

He stands up and extends his hand. I shake it, and then Logan does. Kevin walks past us and out of the room. We follow him back to the front door, where he holds the door open for us.

"The service will start at eleven, but I would ask that you show up to the cemetery twenty minutes early. That's all you need to do though, I'll take care of everything else."

"Thank you," Logan says, shaking Kevin's hand again.

I force a slight smile onto my face and nod to thank him. When we get back in Logan's SUV, he turns to me and takes my hands in his and looks at me. I keep my eyes facing forward. I know that if I look at him right now I'll start crying.

"Are you alright?"

I want to lie and say yes, just so that he doesn't have to carry any more of my burden. I can't bring myself to say it though. I feel like he deserves more than that.

"No, not really."

He squeezes my hand. I finally turn my head and look into his eyes. I can see in his eyes that he wants me to tell him everything.

"I just… I don't know. I still can't believe that all of this is happening. I mean obviously I knew that my parents would die at some point, but I never imagined that one of them would leave and the other would die in such a short amount of time. I feel like I'm falling apart. I don't know how long I can hold it together."

"I'm here for you. Don't ever feel like you can't tell me what's going on. If you need anything, you need to just tell me and I'll do everything within my power to help you. You have to tell me though, I can't guess what you're thinking."

I feel so lucky. He's amazing. I lift his hand to my face and give him a kiss. I really don't know what I would be doing right now if he wasn't here for me.

"Thank you."

I squeeze his hand and kiss it again.

"Let's get out of here," I say. "I'm hungry."

If I think about the days that lay ahead of me, I feel like I can't breathe, but when I remind myself that Logan is here for me… I know that I can do anything. We can do anything.

I look at him and smile. He's my white knight.

CHAPTER TWENTY-TWO

Giving up on the idea of falling back asleep, I finally open my eyes and look at my alarm clock. It's just after six. Ugh. I guess my body is used to waking up early to run.

Now that I think about it, I should go for a run. It might do me some good and maybe I can clear my head a little.

I roll over and look at Logan. He looks like a little boy, lost in a good dream. I don't want to wake him, but I'm starting to feel restless.

I watch him for another five minutes before I decide to finally get up. I slowly ease my way out of bed and get dressed. I grab my shoes and carry them downstairs so that I don't wake him up. I head onto the back deck and sit on the top step and put my sneakers on and take a deep breath. There's a crisp feel to the air. It's beautiful out right now.

I head down the road, toward the center of town. It's still early enough that it's quiet and there's no traffic. I could probably count the number of times, in my life, that I was in downtown Greenville at this time of day, and I always liked it. It's just so serene.

As I run, I start to feel better. Jess was right, I'm

starting to like these morning runs. Well, I don't like the waking up early thing, but I feel so much better, physically.

I turn around as I hit the far end of town, figuring that it will make a good halfway point for my run. The door to Java Stop flings open as I run by and Nancy rushes out. I don't slow down.

"Amy!"

I'm far enough away that I could just ignore her. Instead, I turn around and job back to her.

"Hey, Nancy."

"I'm so sorry. I just heard about what happened to your dad."

I should have just kept going.

"Is there anything I can do?"

Yes, leave me alone. It's one of those moments where I really want to say what I'm thinking and don't, thankfully.

"No, thanks though."

She waves at a passing car.

"When is the service?"

I'm tempted to not tell her. I can't explain why though. Maybe I just don't really feel like having half the town show up.

"It's just the burial, at the cemetery, at eleven tomorrow."

"I'll be there," she says.

I force myself to smile at her. I nod my head in the direction I was headed when she stopped me and she smiles. I start running again. I want to get back before too much time goes by. I don't want Logan to wake up and be worried about where I am.

When I get back, I open the back door and head inside. I was worried about waking Logan, but I can tell by the smell that hits me as I walk in that he's awake... and he's cooking something. What could he have possibly found that's edible?

I walk up behind him while he's at the stove and

wrap my arms around his waist. It feels so good. He turns around, kisses the top of my head and looks into my eyes.

"Good morning," he says.

"Hi."

"How did you sleep?"

"Alright, I guess. You?"

"Like a baby," he says.

I lean my head to the side and peek at the stove.

"It's almost ready, take a seat."

He points at the table with a spatula. The clean table. He's been busy.

I sit down at what used to be my normal seat at the table. Logan comes over with a glass of water and sets it down in front of me.

"I hope water's OK, it's either that or beer."

I let out a short laugh.

"Water is fine."

He smiles at me and turns back to the stove. He opens a few cabinets, until he finds the plates. I bring the cool water to my lips. I drink half the glass in one gulp. I had no idea I was so thirsty.

Logan walks over to the table and sets down our plates and a bottle of maple syrup. Pancakes. I can't even look at him. Did he have to make pancakes? It was really sweet of him to make breakfast, but… I don't know if I can eat them.

I notice that he is still standing and unsure of which seat to take. I look up at him and he meets my gaze with a smile. I force myself to smile back, still out of sorts from the pancakes. I point to the one that used to be Mom's. He smiles at me, pulls the chair out and sits down.

Maybe I'm being stupid. They are just pancakes. Logan passes me the syrup and I coat the pancakes. I hand it back to him and he does the same. I pick up my fork, cut a small piece and put it in my mouth.

It tastes just like the ones my dad used to make. I drop my fork and put my hands on my face as I start to cry. Logan jumps up, rushes over and wraps his arms around my shoulder.

"What is it?"

I shake my head. I can't tell him, he will think I'm an idiot.

"Please, tell me."

"Pancakes. My dad," I say, still crying.

Logan holds me tighter.

"I'm sorry, I had no idea."

I take a deep breath and slowly stop crying.

"It's not your fault, I'm sorry," I say.

I shouldn't have reacted that way. He was trying to do a sweet thing and make me breakfast and I went and ruined it with tears. There probably wasn't anything else to even eat.

Logan grabs both of our plates and puts them on the counter.

"You should eat."

"I'm good, I'm not that hungry."

Logan takes my hand and I get up from the table.

"Let's go upstairs, we need to get ready anyway."

He's right. I mean it's a little early to get ready now, but I don't want to be down here anymore. At least in my room it feels more like me and less like him. Everything I look at down here reminds me of him and the pancakes, even though it was sweet of Logan to make them, it sent me over the edge.

I nod and he leads me out of the kitchen, upstairs, and to my room.

"What are you going to wear?" he says.

I shrug. I really hadn't thought about it before. I guess usually women wear some kind of black dress. Maybe Mom left one behind when she moved out. I know that she had a couple, but I never looked in her closet after she left.

"I have no idea. I don't own a black dress."

"Well, I guess you don't have to wear one."

wear a black dress.

I take a deep breath, trying to calm my racing heart, and I step through the door.

You can do this, Amy.

Everywhere I look, everything reminds me of them. Even the vanity reminds me of my mom. It's where she taught me how to put on makeup. The picture I painted for their wedding anniversary, two years ago, is framed and on the wall over the bed. I see their wedding photo on the dresser and I have to look away. It's just too much.

I take another step and then another. With each one, I feel like some of the weight is lifted from my shoulders.

There are two closets in the room, both side by side. The one on the right was my dad's and the one on the left my mom's. The right door is open and there are clothes falling off the shelves and on the floor. I guess at some point I'm going to have to deal with that, but not right now.

I wish I could just walk out of here forever, right now. It's just not that easy. After today I have to figure out what to do with all of the stuff in the house. And then what about the house? I can't own a house. Not to mention I want to go back to Salem, especially now that I can actually go to State.

I guess I'll have to figure all that out, but first… first I have to get through today and that's not going to be an easy task, even with Logan on my arm.

When I open the door on the left, I'm surprised to see the whole closet is still full. It doesn't look like she took anything, which I find almost hard to believe. She was always very meticulous about her clothes and making sure they were hung by color in the closet.

I find the black section and start to look for a dress. I find one and pull it out. It should work, it's a sort of traditional three-quarter sleeve black dress. It looks like something my mother would wear to a funeral. The strange thing is that I don't ever remember seeing her wear it.

While holding the dress, I start to look through her shoes. I need something black to go with the dress. The shoes Jess gave me definitely won't work, not to mention they aren't really funeral appropriate.

I eventually find a pair of black patent leather flats, pull them out and look inside. They are a six and a half, which is what she wears, unfortunately, but I'm going to have to try and squeeze into them because I don't really have much of a choice.

I look through her shoes for another minute, hoping to find something that might fit better, but can't find anything. Taking the shoes and the dress, I head back to my room.

The door is just barely open and I walk in without giving it a second thought. Logan turns around, with just a pair of boxers on. I close my eyes and spin around.

"Sorry."

Logan starts to laugh.

"It's alright, you didn't see any more than the first time we met."

I guess he's right, I didn't even think of that. I guess at the time, I tried to block that out. Obviously he hasn't forgotten about it.

"It's safe now," he says.

I turn back to him and he now has a T-shirt on and is pulling up his pants. I smile at him and hold up the dress and shoes.

"This is all I could find."

"It looks perfect to me, plus we'll match," he says, smiling at me.

"Could you be any more cute?"

"I can try."

He raises one eyebrow and nods his head slightly. I can barely keep myself from laughing.

CHAPTER TWENTY-THREE

"Here?"

I snap back into reality and look to where Logan is pointing.

"Yeah, that's it."

The cemetery is just on the other side of the church and goes up the hill. There is a parking lot at the bottom and a paved path that leads up to where the plots are. A road runs from the parking lot that just goes to the top and loops back around and it's used by the hearse.

He pulls the SUV into the parking lot of the cemetery. I glance at the clock, it's ten-thirty. We have a few minutes before we needed to show up, but I doubt they would have started without us.

There are a few other cars in the parking lot, none of which I recognize. That's one of the things about a small town, if there was someone here that I knew, I would recognize their car. I doubt that there's another funeral happening today. I wonder who could be here. Maybe one of them belongs to Pastor Evans.

"Are you ready?" Logan says.

No. I don't think that I'll ever be ready for this.

"Sure."

"I know that nothing in your life can prepare you for something like this. Just be strong and you'll get through it and I'll be by your side, the whole time. I promise that everything will be OK."

"Thank you, I appreciate it."

He turns to me and smiles.

"You're welcome," he says.

"I don't think that I would have been able to do this alone. It's so amazing that you're here right now. I feel like things just fell into place with us and we met when we were supposed to. It's really wonderful."

He smiles and takes my hand in his.

"I'm glad that you came into my life. I know that things are crazy right now and you're going through a lot, but I want you to know that I want to be with you and I know that once things settle down, it will get easier."

I squeeze his hand. He's so sweet.

Motion outside of the car catches my attention and we both turn our heads. Another car has pulled into the parking lot and a man gets out who is dressed like a priest. It must be Pastor Evans.

"I guess it's time," I say.

We get out and hold hands as we follow Pastor Evans up the path. As we get near the top, he veers off the path and down a row of plots and stops by the grave, which is already dug and there is a large pile of dirt sitting next to it.

"Pastor Evans?" I say.

"Yes?"

He turns around. He has a kind face and he smiles when he sees us. I can tell that he's not here because he has to be, but because he wants to help people.

"I'm Amy, this is Logan."

He holds out his hand and shakes ours.

"I'm so sorry for your loss."

"Thank you."

"Do you have any questions for me? We have

about ten minutes before we start."

I look at Logan and then back to the Pastor. I shake my head.

"No, I don't think so."

"Alright, just so you know, the casket will arrive in a few minutes and then we will lower it into the ground. After that, I will say a prayer and if you wish to say any words, that will be the time for it."

"Thank you."

He turns his head slightly and looks by us, so Logan and I turn around and see a group of people, maybe fifteen or twenty, coming up the path. I recognize a few of them. Nancy is there as well as three guys from my dad's work. They all stop about ten feet behind us and wait, noticing that we are talking to the Pastor.

A black hearse comes up the road, turns around and backs up to the edge of the road.

"Do you have pallbearers?" Evans says.

"What?"

"Pallbearers? They carry the casket. It's heavy."

"How many do I need?"

"I would say three more, plus him," he says, pointing at Logan.

I look at Logan and he nods. Something else I didn't think of. I look back to the group standing behind us.

"Can three of you be pallbearers?"

The three men from Dad's work step up immediately and walk over to me. I recognize them all, having met them at some point, but I can't seem to remember any of their names.

"Thank you."

They all nod, somber looks on their faces saying that they were more than just co-workers, they were friends.

Logan and the three of them walk to the hearse and I turn back to Pastor Evans. He motions to the growing crowd, asking them to approach the plot so that the ceremony can begin.

"Thank you all for being here today," Evans says.

Kevin, from the mortuary, and a man that looks just like him get out of the hearse, open the back and pull the casket out onto the tailgate.

Now it even seems more real.

The three men and Logan walk up to the casket, each of them takes a corner and they lift it and start to carry it to me. The men from the mortuary follow, each carrying a small bag.

Logan looks solemn. I'm sure everyone here is wondering what his relationship is to my dad.

The pallbearers set the casket down next to the grave. Logan comes back and stands next to me and the other three guys go back to their wives.

Kevin hands his bag to Pastor Evans, and with the other man from the mortuary stands to the side. Pastor Evans opens the bag, takes out a vial of water and removes the top. He stands over the casket and sprinkles the water over the top. He puts the top back in the water and puts it in his pocket.

"At this time, we invite the family of the deceased to say a few words, should they so choose," Pastor Evans says.

I make eye contact with him and nod. He gestures to a spot next to the casket. I walk over and turn to face everyone. I'm actually a little surprised by how many people showed up. I clear my throat and take a deep breath.

"Thank you all for coming. I know that most of you knew my Dad, and that his death shocked this community."

I feel like I can't breathe. I want to cry. I want to be anywhere but here. Everyone is looking at me, waiting for me to say something profound about my dad. Should I tell them how much of an ass he was the last couple months of his life? How he cost me a job and scared me enough that I ran away?

I look at Logan and he smiles at me. I feel calm when I look at him and remember what he said earlier. I just need to get through this and things will get easier.

"My dad… he was a good guy. He wasn't perfect, but you probably all know that."

Out of the corner of my eye I see a black car, with tinted windows, drive up the road and park next to the hearse. I wait for a second, watching to see if anyone gets out, but no one does. I turn my attention back to the funeral.

"He was a good dad and I'm going to miss him terribly."

I know it's my only chance to say what I'm feeling and how mad I am at him. I just can't bring myself to do it. If I'm going to regret something I would rather it be that I didn't say anything than saying something that I remember for the rest of my life and wish I could take back.

Pastor Evans nods to Kevin, who opens the other bag that they brought with them and takes out straps. He and the other man from the mortuary wrap them around the casket. They slide it over the hole and start to lower it into the ground. They detach the straps, pull them out and put them back in the bag before heading back to the hearse.

Pastor Evans stands over the casket, pulls the vial of water and sprinkles some more on it.

"Grant this mercy, O Lord, we beseech Thee, to Thy servant departed, that he may not receive in punishment the requital of his deeds who in desire did keep Thy will, and as the true faith here united him to the company of the faithful, so may Thy mercy unite him above to the choirs of angels. Through Jesus Christ our Lord. Amen."

"Amen," everyone says.

"May his soul and the souls of all the faithful departed through the mercy of God rest in peace," Pastor Evans says.

Tears start to roll down my face as one by one the group of people walks up to me, gives me a hug and gives me their sympathy. When the last of them leaves, Logan wraps his arms around me as I cry. He kisses the top of my head.

"C'mon, let's get out of here," he says.

We hold hands and walk back down the hill to the parking lot. The black car drives by us, almost coming to a stop. When we look at it, the car speeds off and leaves the parking lot.

"That was weird," I say.

"Totally."

We get in Logan's SUV and he pulls out of the parking lot and we head back to the house.

The black car is parked three houses down, facing away from us. It's not unheard of to see a car more than once in Greenville on a given day, since it's such a small town, but something just seems off. Why were they parked at the funeral and now here?

"Are you doing alright?" Logan says, as he parks in the driveway.

"As good as I could possibly be doing right now."

We get out and head inside.

"I get that. Tomorrow will be better."

He's right. I can't think about tomorrow. Today is still staring me in the face.

I get a glass out of the cabinet. While I'm standing at the sink, filling it up, Logan walks into the living room.

"That car just moved," he says.

"Really?"

"Yeah, they are parked across the street now."

I turn off the faucet, set my glass down on the counter and go into the living room. Logan is standing at the window and has the curtain pulled back just enough to peek out. I walk up behind him, put my arms around his waist and look around him. He pulls the curtain back a little more, so that I can see.

Sure enough, the black car from the funeral is parked across the street.

"I wonder what they want," Logan says.

I don't know, but I'm starting to get a bad feeling about it.

"Maybe I should call the cops."

Logan drops the curtain and turns around. He puts a hand on either side of my face and looks into my eyes.

"I'll go see what they want. I'm your man, let me take care of it."

"Are you sure? Do you think it's safe?"

"I'm sure it's fine. This is small town America."

He kisses me on the head again and opens the front door. I watch as he walks down the steps, across the street and up to the car. The back window rolls down and he walks up to it. He leans over. I can hear him talking, but I can't understand what he's saying.

Logan straightens up, shakes his head and turns around. He comes back and I can see the irritation on his face as he climbs the stairs.

"What's wrong?"

He comes inside, closes the door and turns to me.

"It's your mom."

I don't even know what to say. Is it possible? Why would she be here? If she really cared about Dad, she wouldn't have left in the first place.

"Are you sure?"

He nods his head.

"You look just like her. It was weird, I wasn't expecting to be looking at future you."

I'm not sure what to do. She came to the funeral, but she didn't want anyone to know she was there? The only thing I can think of is that she must be ashamed of leaving us and didn't want anyone in town to see her.

"What did she want?"

"She wouldn't tell me. I told her I was your boyfriend and she just stared at me."

Boyfriend? It warms my heart to hear him say that. We hadn't really talked about it yet, but I was hoping that we were at least heading in that direction. He easily could have just told her that he was my friend, but he chose to say boyfriend.

"Ugh."

No part of me even wants to talk to her, or see her. As far as I was concerned, after what she did to us, I didn't care if I ever saw her again.

Logan smiles at me. My disgust with her must be all over my face.

"I know you're mad at her, and you should be, but she's your mother and you just buried your father. Maybe you should just at least go see what she wants."

He's right, of course. She's my only parent, I should at least speak to her. Even if I don't think she really deserves it.

"You're right. I guess I'll just go out there and see what she wants."

"I'll be right here if you need me."

"Thank you… for everything. You've been amazing."

He smiles at me and squeezes my hand. As I turn toward the door, Logan gives me a light smack on the butt and I feel my face turning red. Perfect, just what I need when I have to talk to Mom. I won't be able to think about anything but Logan. He's so freaking cute.

That awful feeling of not being able to breathe comes over me, getting stronger with each step I take toward the ominous black car. I just want to turn around, run back inside and jump into Logan's arms.

I reach the car, the window is still down, and I look inside. It's my mother, but I barely recognize her. Her once long brown hair is now short and blonde. She's wearing designer sunglasses and a black dress that is more revealing than the one I'm wearing.

"That dress looks good on you," she says.

She must know that it used to be hers.

"Why are you here?" I say, ignoring her pseudo compliment.

She lowers her head so that she can see over the top of her sunglasses.

"Don't take that tone with me, young lady."

"Who do you think you are? You left, you left me and you left Dad. What are you doing here?"

"I came to get you."

"What are you talking about?"

She lets out a deep sigh, as if I'm inconveniencing her in some great way.

"I'm taking you back with me, at least until you turn eighteen."

I can't breathe. I want to scream. I open my mouth, but nothing comes out.

"So, go inside and pack your bags and be quick about it, the plane is waiting."

I hate her. She can't make me leave. No way in hell am I going anywhere with her. I turn around and start walking back to the house.

"Amy!"

I ignore her and keep going. I hear the car door close as I reach the porch. Logan opens the door and I run in and slam the door.

"What happened?" he says.

"She said I have to go with her."

His eyes grow wide. He's almost as shocked as I was. She can't do this. As far as I'm concerned the day she left here, she gave up any right toward me as a parent.

"What?"

Before I can answer her, the front door flies open, she barges in and we both turn to look at her.

"Amy, pack your bag. Now."

"I don't have to go with you."

Logan squeezes my hand. I'm not going anywhere.

"Yes, you do actually. As your only parent, I'm responsible for you until you turn eighteen and I can't risk leaving you here."

"I don't believe you."

She looks at Logan, as if he is going to side with her.

"Look," she says. "I don't want this either, trust me, but I don't know what to tell you. You can come back in a month. You just can't be here now. Until your birthday you have to stay with me."

Logan squeezes my hand. I know she's right. The only way I could live on my own is if I was emancipated and that process would take longer than a few weeks. I really don't have much of a choice.

I turn to Logan, my eyes pleading with him to think of another way. I can't leave him, not now. He looks at her.

"Please, don't do this to her. Don't do this to us," Logan says.

She looks at him and for a brief moment I see compassion in her eyes. It fades and she turns back to me.

"Go get your stuff. Don't make me ask you again."

There's no way around it. She won't leave here without me. Logan and I walk upstairs while she waits in the living room. We go into my room and he closes the door behind us.

"What do I do?" I say.

He just looks into my eyes. I can tell by the sadness in his eyes that he knows there is nothing we can do. We both know that I have to go with her, we just don't want to say it. It will seem real if we do.

"You have to go."

Tears form in my eyes. I can't believe this is really

happening. Logan grabs my already packed duffel bags and puts them on the bed. He walks over to me and wraps his hands around my head and lowers his mouth to mine.

He pushes his lips against mine. My tongue darts forward and into his waiting mouth. His tongue touches mine and I can feel a heat building deep in my body. It's like nothing I've ever felt before. It's a perfect kiss.

Logan pulls his head back, darts in for one last peck on my cheek and then takes a step back, holding my hand.

"You're amazing. The moment you can get back here, you do it. I'll be waiting for you."

"I will, I promise. And I'm going to call and text you every day."

"You'd better."

I smile at him. I'm going to miss his touch. His smell. I'm going to miss all of it.

"Amy!"

I'm kind of surprised that it took her this long to yell for me. I wrap my arms around Logan, one last time, and he kisses the top of my head as he runs his hands down my back. I drop my arms and Logan grabs the bags in his left hand.

As we walk downstairs, holding hands, it's over too quick. He gives my hand a final squeeze and we head outside, my with mom in the rear. The trunk of the car opens when we get closer and Logan sets the bags inside.

My mom opens the back door, on the driver's side, and waits for me to get in. I brush my lips against Logan's and get into the car. She gets in after me and slams the door.

"Let's go."

The driver starts the car and pulls away. I turn my head and watch Logan for a brief moment before we turn a corner and he is gone. I can't believe she's doing this to me. I turn my head back around and look out the window. Thankfully she's as quiet as I am.

I miss Logan. My birthday can't come fast enough.

~~~

Thank you for reading Crazy Love. I hope you enjoyed the story and that you will want to read the next book. If you want to join my mailing list, I will send out an email when the next book is released.

http://eepurl.com/xbe7z

Also, if you want to find out more about me or my other books, please visit my website http://www.emmakeene.com

ABOUT THE AUTHOR

I live in beautiful Seattle, WA with my amazing, supportive husband and our two German Shepherds that truly believe it's all about them. I love the rain and it gives me plenty of time to read and write.

CPSIA information can be obtained
at www.ICGtesting.com
Printed in the USA
LVHW010612281118
598504LV00020B/2095/P

9 781494 292508